A Beautiful Struggle

with love &
appreciation,

Lilliana

Books by Lilliana Anderson

Confidante: The Brothel

A Beautiful Struggle

Coming Soon

Confidante: The Escort

A Beautiful Redemption

Confidante: The Madame

For information on upcoming releases visit

http://lillianaanderson.weebly.com

A Beautiful Struggle

Lilliana Anderson

2013

ISBN-13: 978-1481162524

ISBN-10: 1481162527

Design by Ember Designs

Printed by CreateSpace Publishing USA

Dedication –

To Wade

for helping me change the important things

'Sticks and stones are hard on bones,
Aimed with angry art,
Words can sting like anything
But silence breaks the heart.'

Phyllis McGinley, "Ballade of Lost Objects," 1954

Contents

Foreward

This book started off as something very different to what it is now.

Originally, I had planned to try my hand at writing several erotic short stories for a bit of fun. I had started this book as a document titled 'Office Job' and was going to simply write about co-workers romping around the office, wherever they could manage.

However, the characters came alive in my mind and started to tell me that there was more to their story than mere sex. I would wake in the morning and the first thing I would think of would be them.

Still tied up finishing the editing process of Confidante: The Brothel, I was unable to listen to them fully. I felt slightly tortured by them for a while as they stayed in my head and begged me to write them. When Confidante was completed, I took one week off and then entered NaNoWriMo – completing the first draft of A Beautiful Struggle in 22 days. Their story was so fluid in my mind that I just needed to sit and let my fingers flow over the key board.

I sincerely hope you enjoy the story of Katrina, Elliot and David. I know that I enjoyed writing them.

Acknowledgements

First and foremost I must thank all of the Beta readers and Advanced reviewers who agreed to look over this book.

Melissa, Bree, Mia, Jade, Rachel, Sara, Ginnie, GW, Courtney, Crystal & Vicki.

Whether, you loved it, hated it, or just couldn't find the time to read it – I still greatly appreciate the support you gave me, no matter how small.

There is one more reader that I really want to thank separately and that is Pati – she is the Beta Reader Extraordinaire and provided me with invaluable feedback for this book as well as becoming the muse for a sequel idea. Pati, you are magnificent! Thank you, thank you! I hope you like the changes I made since we last conversed.

Another thank you is of course to my editor (WS) for being tough with me and making me rework so much of this book and cut out a lot of superfluous junk.

I also want to thank my family, especially my husband for supporting me while I write. My husband listened to my ideas and gave me great story suggestions, and held my hand while I bit my fingernails nervously while I waited for reviews to come back.

The very last thank you is to you, the person reading right now – you are the whole entire reason that I have worked so hard to create this book. Enjoy.

Prologue

"Oh my god! *Why* are you making me sit through this girly movie?" David complained as the couple on the screen struggled with their attraction to each other yet again.

Laughing at him, I answered, "Because it was my turn to pick – *you* made me sit through that horrible action movie last time, so consider us even."

"Fine," David grumbled. "But I need more beer to get through this, do you want one?"

Shaking my head no, I lifted my legs from his lap so he could stand. I didn't think that my boyfriend Christopher would be happy if he came home from work and I was rolling around on the floor, drunk with David. Actually, David needed to be gone before Christopher got home. They weren't exactly friendly with each other.

I sucked in my breath as I heard the key enter the door and click it open, it was as if the thought had been enough to conjure him.

David spun around and locked eyes with me, his own as wide as mine were. Gulping, I watched as Christopher walked through the front door and prepared myself for the verbal tirade that was sure to follow.

"You're early," I pointed out, my heart thumping loudly as I flicked my worried gaze toward David in the kitchen.

Christopher followed my line of sight, his face darkening as he spotted my friend.

"What the fuck are you doing here?" Christopher bellowed at David, giving him zero chance to respond before he marched towards him, planting the full force of his fist into the side of David's face rocking him back on his heels before he slowly fell.

"No!" I screamed, covering my mouth in horror as I watched David fall to the floor. "What are you doing, Christopher!? Get away from him!"

My protests were futile. As David scrambled to get up, Christopher grabbed the back of his shirt and dragged him to the door, throwing him unceremoniously out into the hallway.

"Stay the fuck away for good this time!" he yelled at David before slamming the door and flicking the lock.

As Christopher turned his attention to me, I stopped breathing but my heart raced.

"You!" he bellowed, I felt the bile rise in my throat as he charged towards me, his face twisted with fury.

Chapter 1

If my life was a movie, it would have been playing Dolly Parton's 'nine to five' as I entered the building in Sydney's Martin Place that housed the law offices of Turner Barlow & Smith. It was my first day as the part-time librarian, actually it was my first job full stop, and I was nervous as hell.

The music would have then come to a screeching halt after I had exited the lift and approached the reception area to introduce myself.

The frosty receptionist - taking an instant disliking to me, that was made painfully obvious; gave me a look that told me I was no better than the crud under her beautifully manicured fingernails.

I have to admit I felt a little intimidated by her looks; she was beautifully made up and very curvaceous - she looked like one of those sexy cartoon pin up girls you see from war time posters, with jet-black hair cascading down over her shoulders and a bust daring to break through her fitted blouse that a flat chested girl like me would pay dearly for.

Despite feeling a little ill at ease by the frostiness of her gaze bearing down on me. I took a deep breath and boldly told her who I was and why I was there. She tilted her head back and looked down her nose at me - a difficult thing to do to someone as tall as me, but she succeeded insurmountably; and told me curtly to sit and wait for the office manager.

Taking a deep breath, I turned and looked at the reception waiting area, sighing when I saw the low-set furniture. I walked towards it wondering how the heck I was going to fold my long legs in some sort of a dignified manner, so I wouldn't flash the office manager when he or she came out. I chose to perch on the edge of a cream leather couch with my knees angled down and legs tucked to the side, imagining that I looked a little like a daddy long legs spider but not having much choice in the matter.

I had applied for this job in the hopes that it would be a foot in the door by the time I graduated. I was two years into studying a humanities/law degree at the University of Western Sydney, Parramatta campus - which was only half an hour's drive away from my home in Cranebrook, one of Sydney's western suburbs.

I was originally born in Penrith (or Penriff, as a lot of people jokingly call it) but my parents had saved as much money as they could to buy a new house and move out to Cranebrook which they considered to be a step up in the world. It wasn't – it's the suburb right next door to Mount Pleasant, home to one of the largest public housing estates in the west.

There was a fair bit of crime in the area, my car had been broken into numerous times, but we had been lucky and never had our house broken into. So, in the grand scheme of things, it was no big deal – petty crime was just something you dealt with when you were a blue-collar family living in an area that housed people both less and more fortunate than you.

The best way for me to travel to work was via train, which took about an hour. I had woken up extremely early that morning as I really wanted to make a good first impression - taking an extraordinary amount of time getting ready, ensuring I looked just right.

I had chosen a black pinstripe skirt that came to my knees with a crimson satin blouse and low heeled black maryjane shoes. I had straightened the natural wave out of my long honey blonde hair so it sat just below my shoulders, wearing enough makeup to cover a scar that ran along my hairline and to give my lips and cheeks a rosy glow.

My goal was to look professional but be comfortable enough to climb ladders while I lugged books up and down the shelves. I thought the effect worked well and was at least feeling good about my looks despite being nervous about my job. I had even caught the earlier train in to the city from Penrith station just to make sure I had plenty of time to navigate my way from Wynyard station to my new workplace on the corner of Martin Place and Phillip St.

I only had to sit awkwardly on the low-set chairs for a few minutes before a small woman who appeared to be in her mid-30s and of Indian origin came out to greet me. "Hello, my name is Priya. I am the office manager," she said extending her hand in greeting. "You must be Katrina."

I immediately rose, dwarfing Priya with my six feet of height, smiled and shook her hand. "Yes, that's me. It's lovely to meet you."

Priya looked up at me and said the first thing most people say upon meeting me, "My, you're a tall one aren't you?" I smiled and nodded to be polite while inwardly rolling my eyes. "Follow me and I will show you around the office."

I did as I was told, following closely behind her and trying to take in as much information about my surroundings as possible.

Priya spoke over her shoulder and pointed things out as we went along, "In here are the conference rooms, you only need to know about them for drinks on Friday nights – there is a social committee that is in charge of all that, you can join if you like. Mary runs it all and should come to talk to you about it at some point today."

We continued down the corridor, past different offices and cubicles. Priya explained that the corner offices were for the partners, and the middle offices were for the junior and senior solicitors. Outside the offices were the personal assistant's cubicles and then there was a row of offices inside for accounts and other support staff. Administration had a cubicle section all of its own, and in the very centre of everything were the filing room, the library and the break room.

"Here is where you will be working," said Priya. I looked at the large room lined with built-in bookcases that reached the ceiling, as well as two rows of smaller bookcases lining the centre. There were two desks against the outer wall with a reference computer on one, and a microfiche reader on the other, in between those was a photocopier.

My own desk was in the corner. It had a low cubicle divider

around it with a computer and an in/out tray that was piled high with mail, law journal updates and microfiche slides.

"Wow, this is bigger than I expected," I stated.

"Not too big I hope," Priya smiled before launching into the next part of my orientation. "Now, you will be responsible for making sure all the books are in the correct place of course, as well fetching any books that people have removed. They have to check the book out, but sometimes they just take it, so you may have to do some hunting at times.

"You will need to stocktake once a fortnight to make sure you have a list of any missing books. Most importantly, you need to keep the law journals up to date; new updates come in regularly."

She pulled an update from my in tray and showed me the instruction sheet that told me what pages to add and take away, I couldn't see myself having difficulties with it. "Also, you have to sort these microfiche into order and then give them to one of our junior solicitors, Elliot; he is responsible for updating the system with those."

"Oh, I thought the microfiche would be in here because the readers are here," I interrupted.

"No, they are kept with the files, but you will get people leaving them in here, sometimes in the reader itself. Just sort them and return them all to Elliot, he will deal with them. He also catalogues the law magazines that get sent to us. I will take you to meet him now so you know where his office is."

Priya led me down the corridor and into an open area, where a group of PA desks were clustered, surrounded by window offices. She came to a stop outside a small windowed office right next to the Partner's, and tapped on the door before opening it. A man in his early 20s looked up from his work revealing the most vivid blue eyes I had ever seen. My breath caught a little as I drank him in. Even through his dress shirt I could see how well muscled he was, his face showing that smattering of stubble I loved on a man. I don't know how else to describe him except to say that he was beautiful; those blue eyes, that full mouth, his light golden-brown hair and those broad shoulders! I felt myself swoon a little but came back to reality when I noticed him arch one of those perfect eyebrows of his at us in question.

"Sorry to interrupt Elliot but I just wanted to introduce you to our new librarian Kat," Priya said.

"Um, Katrina," I said, hating having my name shortened to that of a furry animal.

"Sorry – Katrina," Priya corrected with a slight eye roll.

Elliot didn't speak at first; he just sat there studying me.

My cheeks flushed involuntarily and the discomfort of being stared at caused me to start nervously looking around the room, out of the door; anywhere but at him.

My apparent unease seemed to make him realise he was staring. He quickly cleared his throat and said, "Hello Katrina." His voice was as beautiful as the rest of him, it had a deep rumble to it that sent chills up my spine.

I was trying desperately to be cool, so he didn't notice my immediate attraction. A guy like this must have women swooning all over him, and I wasn't going to let myself be one of them – despite his hotness. I had met guys like him before, and it never ended well.

Despite my efforts, I didn't manage much more than a tight smile, a small nod and a, "Hi, um, uh, Elliot." *You sound like an idiot!* my mind told me. There was a silence after that; nobody said a word and this awkwardness enveloped us like a thick woolen blanket while we all tried not to make eye contact.

I felt like I needed to say something to break the silence,

"Ah…I didn't think a junior would get a window office," I observed, regretting the comment the moment it left my mouth.

Elliot looked over his shoulder at the window behind him and shrugged, "Every solicitor gets one. It comes with the office. Mine is a very small one though." His blue eyes met mine but revealed no emotion. I could imagine that he must have thought I was a complete ditz! I could feel the heat as it rose in my cheeks while moths of embarrassment churned through my stomach.

Priya raised her eyebrows at the exchange, smiled and commented, "Well; this was fun." She ushered me out of his office as she told Elliot, "Just thought you should meet Katrina so you knew what she is doing leaving things on your desk. Enjoy your day Elliot," she gently closed his door and led me back towards the library. "So, your bright-red face tells me you noticed he's a bit of spunk huh?" she said quietly to me when we were far enough away. I tried to act nonchalant and just shrugged my shoulders a little. "Don't get any ideas though, all the girls are after him but he doesn't show interest in any of them. There's a strict no dating policy here and he adheres to it; there's a list of junior solicitors a mile long wanting to work here and I really don't think he is going to risk his job."

"Fair enough," I said, mentally kicking myself for feeling a little disappointed.

"Someone nice to look at though huh? Stops the office being so boring."

"I suppose it does," I answered carefully.

"Well, here we are, back at your new home away from home," she said stopping in front of the library's entrance, "If you need anything today, don't hesitate to call me."

I nodded that I would and thanked her for the tour before entering the library to start work. As I flipped through the items in my tray, I couldn't imagine that I would need to call Priya for help, everything was very basic - all I had to do was sort books, microfiche and follow a simple instruction sheet for the law journal updates; take out page 22, insert new page 22 - I'd be fine.

Alone, I took some time to look around my new work space, so I could take it all in. It felt peaceful being surrounded by books – the colours helped add to the calming effect; pistachio green for the small spaces of wall and a dim grey for the bookcases. There was only one wall without book shelves and that was the one with the desks, microfiche machine and photo copier. That wall had a large window taking up the top half of it so you could see inside as you walked past.

The partition that separated my desk from the rest of the room, was a similar grey to the book cases with tiny flecks of white and black to add some contrast. The desk itself was a light grey, as were the other desks in the room. All the chairs were black padded swivel desk chairs – they looked comfy enough. I walked to the one situated behind my desk and sat down to test it out, adjusting the height setting to suit me. I twisted lightly from side to side and grinned to myself as an idea came to me, I peeked over my partition to make sure I was still alone and then tucked my legs in tight and spun around on my chair in sheer childish abandon. I placed my hands on the desk to stop the spinning and sighed happily; it was exciting to have my own space within an office – I felt a little like a girl playing dress up though.

I reached out to my 'in' pile and took the law update that Priya had shown me, got up and collected the folder it belonged in and started to find and replace the pages required. I hadn't gotten much work done before a woman a few years older than me with chestnut brown hair, and a Mediterranean complexion came in to introduce herself.

"Hi, you must be Katrina! I'm Mary, Francis's PA - you may have seen him on your tour – I'm the head of the social committee!" she announced it to me like there should have been a *TaDa!* at the end of it, she seemed very peppy. "I thought I would pop in to welcome you to Turner, Barlow and Smith, and also, to give you a rundown of the things we like to do here."

I sat silently listening to her chatter on about Friday drinks and other various social activities that come up throughout the year. I told her that I would try to make it to the next Friday night drinks but wasn't really sure if I had anything on yet.

"No worries, it would be great if you came even if it was only half an hour," she smiled.

"Ok, I'll make sure I at least do that," I said feeling the pressure to fit in.

"So um, this is your first job is it?"

"Yeah, very first," I admitted.

"I am sure you will like it here, there's a pretty good group of people around. I mean, you get your cliques like you do everywhere but mostly people are pretty nice. I'll see you around, if not, on Friday ok?" she said as she turned to leave and practically bounced out the door.

"Sounds great," I called after her, smiling weakly. I really didn't know if I was a Friday night drinks person, but I figured I had better show my face if I wanted to make any friends here.

After I got a little more work done I left the library to go and get a coffee at morning tea time. There were two PA desks outside the offices in front of the library door, and one of the girls, a small, slightly rotund girl with a friendly face and dirty blonde hair tied up in a bouncy ponytail, got up as I approached.

"Hi there, I'm Kayley," she said in an Irish accent.

"Katrina," I replied and we shook hands briefly.

"I'm Greg's PA. He's a bit creepy," she whispered.

"Is he?" My eyes skittered around nervously, I wasn't really sure I should be having this conversation.

"Yeah, sometimes I go in there to drop something off, and he is under his desk."

"Ok... doing what?"

"Exactly! That's the part I find creepy."

I laughed, my concern ebbing away, as we started to talk

about how long she had been working there and what some of the other girls were like.

When we reached the kitchen, I met Anne and Carl, who were the filing clerks, as well as Albina and Joanne, who were both PAs as well. I couldn't help but notice that most of the people in the break room were all support staff. Any solicitors who came in made their coffee or tea, uttered some small talk and then left.

Kayley must have noticed me looking around and read my confused expression. "They don't really associate too much with all of us Plebs. The younger ones do sometimes, but they generally just talk to each other and hang out in their offices." She handed me a cup for my coffee, and we moved along the line of people waiting for the water heater. "Although I wish this one would hang around a bit more," she added as her eyes moved to the doorway, I looked around as Elliot walked in. He nodded and said hello to a couple of people but mostly stood there quietly, waiting for his turn for coffee, tea or whatever his chosen refreshment was.

One of the other PAs moved towards him and started a conversation. I was stupidly standing there, openly watching him when he realised and looked at me, stopping mid-sentence for just a beat, this however, caused the girl who was talking to him to glance over her shoulder at a now red faced me. She squinted her eyes, shooting daggers in my direction, flicked her long honey streaked hair over her shoulder and continued her conversation with Elliot.

Kayley leaned into me and said, "He's pretty delicious huh? The one talking to him is Beth, she's his PA and thinks she has dibs on him. But every woman here is lusting after the man. He is devine! Just look at that body! And the hair, the eyes! I could go on," she sighed.

I tore my eyes away from him and tried to focus on Kayley, "Priya told me there's a 'no dating' policy here."

"That doesn't stop anyone," Albina added, eyeing Elliot up and down like he was a piece of meat, "It wouldn't stop me if I got a chance with him anyway." She let out an appreciative growl, and I grinned, enjoying her audaciousness but refusing to look towards Elliot again.

The line moved along at a steady pace, and we all took our drinks to one of the tables inside the break room. At our table was Anne, Carl, Albina, Joanne – who prefers to be called 'Jo'; Kayley and myself. It kind of felt like a scene from a high school movie were a group swoops in and claims the new girl - they all seemed nice though, and were filling me in on some of the office happenings. I found out that the IT guy was having an affair with one of the admin girls, they thought no one knew but weren't very good at pretending nothing was happening, no one cared enough to report them though, so they were left to it.

As is usual with a new person, they were very interested in my life, and wanted to know if I had a boyfriend and what I did with my spare time. I told them I had recently broken up with a guy I lived with for 3 months, and that I trained for triathlons around work and my law degree at university.

"So you want to be one of them," Carl commented.

"I suppose, but I'll make sure I'm still kind to the little plebs," I replied with a smile.

Chapter 2

When morning tea was over, Kayley and I walked back to our area of the office. "Do you want to have lunch with us? We don't do anything special, just gasbag in the break room while we eat and maybe go for a walk, and do a bit of shopping in Pitt St. It would be great if you could come," she offered.

"I really would love to," I answered genuinely, "but I am actually going out to lunch with a friend today."

"Ok, never mind, maybe another time then," she said as she sat down at her desk, and I continued on to the library.

I managed to work steadily until lunch and was excited to grab my bag and get out of the office for a while to have lunch with my best friend David, we have known each other our whole schooling lives and are both studying together at Uni. He was the one that had the idea of getting entry jobs in law firms while we were at university to get our foot in the door. He works a couple of blocks away from me as a filing clerk, so we figured meeting for lunch would be a great way to celebrate us both working now.

Just as I was about to leave the library I was held up by one of the solicitors asking me where a particular book was, it wasn't in the library, so I had to chase it down. In truth, it only took about ten minutes, but I was feeling really bummed that I was then running late to meet David.

I rushed towards the lifts and could see the doors starting to close of a cab that was on its way down, so I ran for it – jumping through the shrinking gap before it got too small for me to fit through.

"Whoa Indiana Jones! I think you left your hat out there!" said the only other person inside the elevator. I sucked in my breath when I noticed it was Elliot. He was leaning against the side of the car smiling his sexy and very amused grin at me. He seemed really friendly – a stark contrast of the stoic man I'd met earlier that day. I actually looked over my shoulder to check he was talking to me. Seeing no-one else, I responded with raised eyebrows.

His brilliant blue eyes were dancing as he clarified, "You know - Indiana Jones? He just makes it under a door and then reaches back for his hat?" I shook my head, and he laughed putting his hands on either side of his head like his head might explode. I gulped as I noted the curve of his bicep through his shirt, "Oh my god! I can't believe you haven't seen that!"

I shrugged my shoulders and offered, "Sorry?"

He was still laughing as shook his head, "No worries; it's just a classic film – you should watch it some time."

"I'll be sure to put that on my to-do list," I told him.

"You should," he put his hands in his pockets and focused on the numbers as they counted towards the ground floor.

Standing close to Elliot, I noticed his height – I guessed he was around 6'3" as he was just a notch above me in my low heels. Gorgeous and tall, I was practically a puddle at his feet. I could feel my body humming with attraction. It felt like there was some sort of force that was trying to pull me towards him. I wondered if he was feeling it too as images of him hot, sweaty and naked flashed through my mind. *Don't think like that!* I chastised myself, not wanting to fall prey to my hormones and make a fool of myself.

Despite the 'no dating' rule stating that I shouldn't act on my attraction, I didn't have time for men in my life. I had recently gotten out of a relationship and had no inclination to start another one – I needed to focus on my sport, my studies and my work; which I thought was more than enough for one girl.

"How's your first day going?" his rumbling baritone invaded my thoughts and snapped me to attention.

"Huh? Oh, Not too bad!" I answered quickly, "just trying to figure my way around."

"It's not so hard. The office is really just a big circle, if you keep going eventually you'll work out where you are," he said as the elevator doors chimed open. "I'll see you around Katrina. That was a pretty cool elevator entrance, it made my day," he beamed at me, and I blushed uncontrollably.

He lifted his hand in a wave as he left. I lingered back in the elevator bay and shamelessly watched him walk away until David placed his head next to mine.

"Who are we looking at?" he whispered.

I blinked away my erotic thoughts of Elliot and turned to David. "Nobody," I answered coyly.

"Nobody huh? I wish you looked at me like I was nobody then. I wouldn't mind doing whatever was in your mind making your cheeks all pink like that," he teased.

I swatted him on the arm. "Get your mind out of the gutter and come and get lunch with me. We've lost 15mins already."

"As you wish my dear Trina," he said wiggling his eyebrows up and down comically, he took my arm and linked it with his as we set off across the street to the nearest food court and have a quick chat and an even quicker meal.

David's usually pretty popular with the ladies, and I noticed a few girls from my office in the food court looking at him with interest. In my heels, he's the exact same height as me. He's pretty easy on the eyes, with sandy blond hair and blue eyes that crinkle shut when he smiles his dashingly dimpled smile. Many a girl has fallen prey to that smile of his, and it has gotten him both in and out of trouble more than once. He is fairly fit, with a lean and wirey build with broad shoulders and a small waist. Occasionally, he trains with me, always holding his own fitness wise.

His features are fairly similar to my own. We're often mistaken for brother and sister, second only to being mistaken for a couple - something that neither of us really wanted to cross the line into; a good thing for our friendship as David tended to have a new girl on his arm every week, and I tended to be more of a long term relationship kind of girl.

"So, are you going to tell me who that guy was you were perving on before?"

I rolled my eyes, knowing that if I didn't tell David he would tease me mercifully until I gave up the information, "It was Elliot. He's the office 'hottie' that all the girls drool over."

"How about you? Are you all of the girls? Because that's what it looked like to me."

"He's hot yeah, and I admit that I was perving but I'm not going to make a fool of myself going after some guy I can't have."

"Who says you can't have him?"

"Um! The fact that there is an office full of gorgeous girls in there, and he hasn't dated one of them," I said all indignant.

"Maybe he's gay?" countered David.

"No, I don't think so. There's a 'no dating' policy."

"That sucks! Where's the fun in that?"

I laughed at this. "We can't all be Mister Sex in the Filing Room with the Receptionist!"

"Hey, I'm all about the pleasure," he said with a cocky half grin on his face.

"I don't know how you get all of those girls to sleep with you, if they knew you like I do they'd run a mile."

"Is that so?"

"Yeah that's so," I told him only half-seriously. Truthfully, I thought that any girl that could hold David's interest for more than ten minutes would find herself a very lucky woman.

He laughed and threw his scrunched up napkin on his tray and looked around the food court, watching the people moving around us. I turned my thoughts inward for a moment before bringing the subject back to me again.

"All joking aside David, I still don't think I'm ready to start dating yet."

His face went sombre as he returned his attention to me. "I know you're not Trina," he reached across the table and squeezed my hand. "I'm sorry for teasing you about Elliot. I wasn't thinking."

I blinked back the emotion that was suddenly prickling the back of my eyes.

"It's fine. You didn't do anything wrong. I'm the one that needs to let go and move on," I took a deep breath and put a smile on my face, pulling my hand away from his. "Besides, a bit of harmless perving on a guy I can't have seems pretty safe to me."

David looked at me with an assessing gaze, "There's no guy on this earth you couldn't have Katrina. You don't give yourself enough credit," he cleared his throat and pushed his chair back, assuming the usual jovial persona that he likes to present to the world. I felt sure that his mother, and myself were the only ones who ever got to see David being serious.

"Well," he said. "I hate to leave the company of a beautiful woman, but I need to get back."

Flicking my hand down, I said, "Oh! That's what you say to all the girls!" in a mock sexy voice.

He shrugged and smiled at me as he started to walk away with his tray, he seemed to remember something and paused mid turn, spinning slightly on his heels before turning to face me again. That's when I noticed something, "Are you wearing hi tops?" I commented, surprised to see them sticking out of the bottom of a pair of dark grey dress pants.

He gave me a half smile that showed his dimple on only one side, "What can I say – they're comfy...Hey, you want to hit the town on Friday night? We haven't been out in the city for ages," he asked.

"I do, but I have to go to drinks at work for a bit beforehand. The social committee chick was pressuring me so it seems pretty important - I will have a drink there and then meet up with you, ok?"

"Sure, I'll email or text you so you know where to meet me."

"Sounds good," I said, standing to leave myself. We hugged good bye, giving each other a cheek kiss before we headed off to our respective jobs.

The lift was more crowded on my way back up to the office; the snooty receptionist was in there with Elliot's PA, Beth as well as maybe ten other people from other floors.

The receptionist turned to me and said, "So was that your boyfriend I saw you having lunch with?"

I frowned and looked at her, not understanding how we went from frosty glares to questions about my personal life so quickly – I didn't even know her name.

Taking my frown for incomprehension, she repeated herself

slowly, "I said – was… that… your… boyfriend?"

"I heard you," I replied. "I'm just not clear on why you're asking me."

She narrowed her eyes and pursed her lips while she exchanged glances with Beth. Beth smiled charmingly, in her stiletto heels, she was a half a head shorter than I was, her skin was creamy and flawless; she looked like a porcelain doll with large hazel eyes, full lips and a heart-shaped face. She was dressed impeccably and had a very slim build, looking like she just stepped out of a magazine ad.

"Let's try this again," she said. "Hi, I'm Beth, and this is Bianca." She held out her hand to shake mine, and I reluctantly took it.

"Katrina," I said cooly, not at all comfortable in this situation.

"I'm Elliot's PA and Bianca, as you probably already know is the receptionist."

I nodded, confirming I did indeed, already know.

"Forgive Bianca, she just saw you with a guy at lunch time and was wondering who he was. No harm intended."

"I'm sure," I said warily, there was something about these two that set my internal alarms off. I didn't like them. "To answer your question - no, he's not my boyfriend."

"Oh, so he's your brother?" Bianca probed.

"Why is this so important to you?" I asked, willing the lift to travel faster so I could escape this conversation.

"Just curious - he's a good-looking guy, I wanted to know if he was fair game; That's all," she said challenging me with her eyes.

I narrowed my eyes a little. "He's not my brother or my boyfriend, and I don't discuss his 'game'. It's none of my business."

Beth and Bianca once again exchanged glances as the elevator opened, and I was granted the freedom to walk straight back to my desk instead of continuing a conversation with those two.

I'm not stupid and I knew Bianca was interested in David, but I'm not his pimp. I don't do set ups – he's perfectly capable of finding girls on his own.

I let out an exasperated sigh as I plonked down onto my chair. Happy to move on from the elevator interrogation, I checked my emails and started sorting through my 'in' tray again.

The rest of the day was pretty uneventful, but I was happy to go home even if that meant enduring the million and one questions my mother was going to ask me about my first day.

"How was it?" she asked the moment I stepped through the front door. I swear she must have been staking it out.

"It was alright, busy and a little overwhelming but ok."

"Did you meet any new people?" she asked.

"Of course she did mum! It was her first day and there would have been an office full of people she hadn't met before!" my older brother chimed in.

I smiled at my mum. I knew she was just excited for me. She had never worked before and found the idea of me working in an office very glamorous.

"I met everyone briefly but clicked fairly well with a small group; they were nice," I said squeezing her arm. "I'm just going to get changed ok?"

"Did you meet any nice boys?" she asked hopefully.

"Mum," I replied in warning.

"I just think you should try moving on. Was there anyone there you might like?"

"Get off her back Mum!" my brother called out. "She's not ready alright."

"Thank you Tom," I called out gratefully. My brother was annoying, but at least he stuck up for me.

"You're welcome. You'll owe me later."

I rolled my eyes at him and looked at my mother, giving her a tight smile, "Can you leave the 'boy thing' alone please. I don't want to date right now."

"Yes but if you'd just move on, have a bit of fun, you might forget," she pleaded.

"I've already forgotten, see!" I gave her the biggest happiest smile I could muster.

She smiled back at me, a sadness in her eyes. "Are you going training?"

"Yes, I will just get changed and head out."

"Oh… ok."

"What does that mean?"

"I just thought we could talk more about your first day."

"There's nothing much more to say mum, it really wasn't that exciting."

"Get off her back!" my brother yelled again.

"Sorry," my mum said quietly.

"It's fine. I just want to get a ride in before I call it a day."

The front door opened and my dad walked in. "Hello family!" he called out as he did every time he came home.

We all called out 'hi' in unison with varying degrees of excitement, "How was your first-day kiddo?" he asked as he walked past me into the kitchen to search the fridge for a cold beer.

"Pretty good – I was just going to get changed to go for a ride."

"Ok, see you when you get back."

I went into my room and got changed into my riding gear. I could hear mum telling my dad that she couldn't understand why he didn't ask me more questions; 'pretty good' could mean anything she told him. I couldn't quite hear what his answer was, but I managed to get out of the house without any further questioning so I could go on my ride.

I loved the peace that training gave me, whether it was going for a run, a cycle, a swim or doing weights, I felt calm when I was working hard. It's like my brain stopped, and I didn't have any worries left. It was tranquillity at its best for me.

After a couple of hours I went home, ate, showered, dodged more questions and flopped into bed. I had uni the next day and caught up on some of my readings before I drifted off. I was working Monday, Wednesday, Friday and at university on Tuesday and Thursday as well as training most days. I was really going to have to work hard to keep on top of everything.

Chapter 3

It was Wednesday, and I was back at work. The office was very quiet all around, I had said a quick hello to Kayley on my way to my desk, but other than that, I hadn't seen anyone. At morning tea I sat with the same people I did on Monday and once again refused lunch, saying that I wanted to run.

"You're very dedicated," said Albina looking me up and down; I'm not a particularly curvaceous woman. I'm primarily muscle and sinew, but that comes with the amount of training that I do and a careful diet. I felt a little self-conscious under her scrutiny as I regularly wished I was more busty and had a bit more of a curve to my hips, so I just shrugged my response and excused myself from the table in the break room.

"But we still have ten minutes!" said Kayley. "Sit and talk to us."

"I can't. I really want to do a bit of uni reading before the break is over."

"Oh, ok, I *guess* that's a good enough reason to go," she smiled cheekily.

As I approached the library, I could see that someone was in there through the internal window. Walking closer, I realised that 'someone' was Elliot. My stupid stomach got all jittery despite me wishing I didn't react to him. I just couldn't help it - he was a beautiful figure to behold – especially from behind. All lean muscle showing through the tailoring of his pants and shirt, it was enough to make a girl sigh out loud – which I nearly did!

He was intently looking through one of the law volumes; he had it sitting on top of the low book cases that lined the middle of the room while he stood with his left leg crossed behind his right, and his shirt sleeves rolled up exposing his muscled forearms while he leaned over the book in concentration.

He turned around when I entered the room. I smiled and said, "Hi, you look busy," to him feeling a little more comfortable around him after chatting in the lift the other day. In return, he gave me a blank impassive face before turning back to his reading.

Wow, talk about the cold shoulder, I thought to myself as I took my seat. I put on my glasses and took out my uni reader.

I could still see Elliot where he was standing and snuck a glance at him from the side of the partition. He was continuing to lean over the book ignoring me. *Did I imagine talking to him Monday?* I didn't think I did, and David saw him as well so it couldn't have been my imagination. I frowned a little while I was looking at him and unluckily for me, he caught me. I quickly flitted my eyes back down to my reading but my cheeks betrayed me as I felt the heat rise in my face, I must have looked like a complete idiot sitting there frowning at him!

I picked up my yellow highlighter so I looked busy and started marking random sections of text in my book, I figured if I looked interested enough in what I was doing, he might just think I was frowning about my work and not at him.

Every sound in the room seemed amplified, especially my own – I could hear my heart beating in my ears, and I seemed to be breathing so loudly that it filled the room.

Above my noises, I could hear the fabric of Elliot's shirt as he moved to turn the very loud page. I tried to still my breathing to calm myself when I heard him close the book and slide it back onto the shelf.

I kept my head down turning pages and pretending to read, highlighting here and there but still focused on him. In my peripheral, I could see him start to walk towards me. I tried really hard to look too busy to notice him; highlight, highlight, thoughtful expression, page turn.

"Katrina?" he said briskly to get my attention when he was near my desk.

I looked up with feigned surprise and said, "Oh hi! Um, Evan is it? What can I do for you?"

He looked a little taken aback when I got his name wrong and started to fumble his words, "Uh, it's um... Elliot actually, I, uh, just wanted to ask you if you had any microfiche for me," he pointed to the sorted pile on my desk. "I figured since I was here I would grab them to save you walking them over to um... my office," his hand flew up, and he rubbed the back of his stylishly messy hair uneasily and gave me a slightly sheepish grin.

"Oh of course, thanks," I replied handing him the pile I had finished with earlier.

"Thank you," he said taking them, he turned slowly, then hesitated. "Uh, bye Katrina, and thanks again for these." He held up the pile of microfiche and started for the door.

I sat there watching him leave, feeling very impressed with

myself. I pulled off the 'deep in thought act' and actually made Mr Hotstuff himself get a little tongue-tied – I guess he wasn't used to women 'forgetting' his name.

Kayley walked in with a conspiratorial grin on her face. "What was that about?" she asked in a low voice.

"What was what about?" I said indifferently.

"Don't play all coy, Elliot just walked out of here with a very confused look on his face. What did you say to him?" she asked with her hands on her hips.

"Nothing, he was looking at a book and then asked me for the microfiche, so I gave them to him."

"Yes, but what did you say?"

"I said 'Thanks'."

"You said 'Thanks'? That's all?"

"That's all."

"Hmmm, if you say so," she said looking at me suspiciously. "I just haven't seen the cool, calm and collected Elliot look confused like that before."

"I don't know what to tell you Kayley, maybe he read something confusing."

"Hmm maybe… alright, I have to get back to work. I'll see you later," she said as she left the library and went back to her desk.

I closed my uni reader and put it back in my bag to start on some more law book updates, smiling to myself about the look on Elliot's face when I called him Evan. *That'll teach him to be rude when someone says 'hi',* I thought to myself.

At lunch time, I wanted to run in the Botanic Gardens. It was the beginning of August; spring had come to the city, and the gardens would be beautiful to run through.

It was a five-minute walk from work to the gardens closest entrance, so I decided to jog and use it as my warm up. I stopped just after I arrived to stretch in front of one of those signs that give you a bit of information on the plants nearby.

Looking around, I could see quite a few people in the park. Some were just sitting on the grass eating their lunch and enjoying the sun, others were in the distance, doing tai chi and I could see a couple of women with a personal trainer doing burpees and not looking very happy about it.

The running track was dotted with people who all had the same idea as I did. I shook out my legs a little as I checked my watch for time – I figured I could run for 15 minutes in one direction and then turn around so I had enough time to get back to the office, shower and return to my desk before the hour was up.

"Katrina?" a newly familiar male voice said behind me. I turned around and came face to face with Elliot.

I couldn't help myself and asked, "Are you following me Evan?" with a cheeky lopsided smile on my face.

Elliot laughed, "No. I'm not following you. I work out most days; I go a bit stir crazy sitting behind a desk all day … and you know it's Elliot right?"

"I don't know about that," I laughed sarcastically. "You see, there's this guy who works in my office called Elliot. He's a bit of an arsehat, grunts at people when they say hi - he looks a lot like you, and I was confused because I thought he was the same friendly guy I was talking to in the lift on Monday; but alas, he was not – it was some guy who I'm assuming is your evil twin." I said all of this with a straight face and my hands on my hips.

He laughed at this half amused and a little uneasy, "Sorry about that, I just try to keep things pretty strict at work; I don't like being the subject of office gossip. So don't take offence if I don't stop to chat, I've been working there a while, and it's best to keep to yourself around those people."

"Ok… how do you know I'm not 'those people'?"

"I don't, just a hunch. You running?" he asked as he started to jog backwards along the path. I took a deep breath as I eyed him up and down, he was wearing running shorts and a quick-dry singlet, giving me a perfect view of how well sculpted his arms, and legs were. My head spun a little as those dirty images flashed through my mind again, *Get a grip!* I told myself, turning my focus onto the matter at hand.

"Yeah I'm running, are you sure you can be seen with me?" I questioned, pressing *start* for the timer on my watch before I ran to catch up.

"This isn't the office, and I don't normally see any of the gossip mongers out here anyway."

"I guess they're all too busy gossiping," I supposed.

"I guess so," he agreed, and we fell into an easy pace side by side, occasionally brushing against each other - I had to force myself to focus so my knees didn't buckle from the bolt of lust that shot through my body every time we made contact – was he doing this on purpose?

Focus Katrina, you're an athlete, and he's a guy you can't have and you don't want – stop being ridiculous! I felt angry with myself that every time I saw Elliot, I would start imagining him naked… and on top of me… underneath me… *stop it!*

"So why are you running? Do you just like it or are you in training for something?"

"Huh?... oh, I do triathlons," I told him quickly, hoping he wasn't reading my thoughts.

"Ah, explains why you've got such a good pace."

"Oh yeah? Thought you'd have to slow down running with a girl huh?"

"I did actually. So you any good at triathlons?"

"I'm decent. I do sprint distance, and I've been in under 19s until now, so I have never really had to race against the big guns of the sport. But I have a hefty stash of medals hanging up at home. Did you ever do any sport or do you just work out for fun?"

"I used to do kayaking in my late teens and early twenties. I was ok at it. I wish I had have been good enough to compete at worlds or even the Olympics, but I barely made it to nationals. So what about you? Will you be trying out next Olympics? You'd still be young enough, wouldn't you?"

"If that's your way of fishing for my age, I'm 20," I smiled, giving him a sidelong glance, "and as far as the Olympics go - it depends on if I'm still competing; It'd be pretty awesome to make it though."

"I know wouldn't it? Nationals were amazing so the Olympics would be off the charts compared."

"And you'd have every sport from so many different countries all in together. Imagine the after party!"

"Ah, the after party – they're the best part!"

"They are," I agreed. We continued to run and chat, until my timer went off. Turns out, Elliot is a really nice guy, and if I could just get past visualising him naked all the time – we could actually be friends.

"What's that for?"

"It's to tell me to turn around so I can get back in time," I answered stopping but jogging on the spot. He did the same and looked at his own watch frowning.

"There's still almost half an hour until the end of lunch, another five minutes, and we will loop around," he told me moving his arm in an arching motion to demonstrate, causing his muscles to flex and my mouth to go dry.

"I want to have a shower and what not. It's fine for you to rush back and rinse off - you don't need to put your make up back on," I called out as I started to run away from him.

"Neither do you. You'd still look great without it," he called out after me.

I laughed, "That's not helping," I called back.

Elliot stopped running on the spot and held his arms out to the side. "Helping what?"

Helping me not visualise you naked! "Good bye Evan," I called over my shoulder, before running back to the office, leaving him to finish the circuit on his own.

***

I walked the last stretch along Phillip St leading to my office for a cool down and did a quick stretch before going inside to ride the elevator back up to my floor. There were maybe 15 people waiting for the next one to arrive, and I wasn't very excited when I saw that Bianca was one of them. She of course noticed me straight away.

"Oh, it's you. I thought you were a man! What *are* you wearing?" she sneared, looking at my running gear like it was covered in cockroaches.

I took up the challenge and looked at her, slowly sliding my eyes over her clothing and down to her shoes with an unimpressed look on my face.

She rolled her eyes and huffed out some air. "Why don't you use the gym upstairs like everyone else so we don't have to look at you like that?"

"I'll tell you what Bianca," I levelled with her, already tired of her horrible attitude towards me. "Why don't you go and fuck yourself?"

Her mouth fell open, and I could hear some muffled snickers from the people waiting around us. She narrowed her eyes and was perhaps going to say something in retort, but the chime signalling the arrival of the elevator cab pinged causing a surge forward of the people waiting around us.

We both joined them in the cab in opposite corners and when the doors opened she was quick to storm out in front of me. I pretended not to notice and made my way to the bathrooms to shower and change before my lunch break was over.

The glory of watching her mouth fall open faded quickly, and I regretted my outburst and wished I could learn to keep my mouth shut. As satisfying as telling her where to go was, it wasn't something I should be doing in a work environment.

Chapter 4

"Hi Mrs Mahoney," David called as he sauntered into the kitchen where I was standing talking to my mother. I was drinking a glass of water, and she was busy cooking the pasta to go with the cabonara sauce she had prepared for dinner. He walked over and kissed her on the cheek and then leaned over and did the same to me.

He stood next to me and leaned up against the kitchen bench, stealing a piece of garlic bread. "So what are we talking about?" he wanted to know.

"Hello David, I was just about to tell Katrina that I played tennis today," my mother informed us.

"You did? That's great! Are you going to keep going?" I asked in response, pleased that she was getting out of the house. She used to play tennis when my brother and I were young; I remembered having a great time hanging out with all the other kids while the mothers played and chatted, but she gave up due to wrist problems, became a home body and never went back to it.

"I will, I think. I'm not sure yet. I will see how my wrist feels tomorrow… Although I did meet the mother of someone you might know from work."

"Really? What a small world – although, I'm not sure if I'll know them, I haven't even met everyone yet."

"Well, her name is Kathy Roberts, and her son's name is Elliot - she said he was a junior solicitor there."

I took a steady sip to try and mask my surprise at hearing her say Elliot's name. David looked at me, recognising the name also, and I shot him a warning glance. I had to think carefully about how I responded as my mother had always had a tendency to see relationship potential where there wasn't any, she'd never really gotten off my back about how much time I spent with David.

She picked up a colander and set it inside the sink, pausing to look at me, "Do you know him?"

Placing my glass on the bench, I said, "I think so, I met one person called Elliot on my office tour. I'm not sure what he does though."

Happy with my answer, she collected the pot and started to pour the pasta into the colander to strain it. "His mother is very nice. She invited me to a lunch with all the tennis girls next weekend – I think I might go."

"That sounds like a lot of fun Mrs M!" David told her. "Would you like me to take the bread and bowls to the table?"

"That would be lovely David," she smiled after him. "I don't know why you two aren't a couple Katrina, you spend so much time together anyway."

"Mum!" I admonished her.

"What? He's such a lovely boy. I don't understand you two."

"I couldn't date David, even if I wanted to – he sticks his dick into a new girl every night!"

"You bitch!" David laughed, as he threw a piece of garlic bread at me. With lightning reflexes, I caught it and took a bite, sticking my tongue out at him as I did.

"I don't believe that," said my mother, "he spends most nights here, so he can't be sticking his… as you put it – dick in a new girl every night."

David and I burst out laughing at my usually very straight mother swearing and left her in the kitchen to finish setting the table for dinner.

"Where's your dad and Tom?" David asked me.

I lowered my voice to a whisper, "Dads at work and Tom is out with his girlfriend who mum and dad don't know about so shhhhh!"

"Is she hot?"

"I don't know. I haven't met her yet."

"Haven't met who yet?" my mother asked as she walked into the dining room carrying a serving dish full of pasta.

"Here mum, give that to me," I offered, reaching out for the bowl.

"Thanks, so who haven't you met?" she asked again.

"Oh…just the big boss at work," I lied as I took my seat at the table. We all began to eat and talk about safe topics, like work, university and my training.

However, sensing an untold story my mother asked, "So are you thinking of starting to date again Katrina? Surely there's a nice young man at the office you could go out with."

"I'm not interested in anyone right now mum," I told her, immediately annoyed.

She turned to David to try to enlist his influence on me, "Don't you think she should start dating again? I'm just concerned that she will miss out on the right guy because she is worried about what happened with Christopher."

"Mum!"

David carefully looked between my mother and I before he answered. "Um…I think she's only 20 Mrs M. She has plenty of time - I know there's no way I'm settling down right now," he told her through a mouth full of food.

"Yes but she's very mature for her age. I don't want her to be turned off men just because of one bad decision."

That pissed me off, "*One* bad decision? Mum! Please leave this alone – I only moved in with Christopher because *you* pushed me to! I wanted to wait until I was at least finished uni before moving in, but you insisted that I shouldn't wait. Seriously mum, stop trying to marry me off! If you don't want me living here again – that's fine, I will look into campus housing tomorrow."

"That's not what I am saying Katrina! I am happy that you're home, but I don't want you to end up like your brother and be nearly 30, still at home and no partner in your life!"

David, very sensibly, kept his head down and shovelled food into his mouth.

"Mum, it's my life – please let me live it. I don't need you to push me again, especially after what happened."

A wounded expression fixed itself on my mother's face, "How could I have known what Christopher was like? You didn't know yourself. Please don't put that on me."

"Why not? It's the truth - If you hadn't have pushed me, David and I wouldn't have been there and none of this," I held up my forearms and flashed my hands at my face and shoulder, "would have ever happened."

"Katrina, that's not fair," David put in.

"It might not be fair, but you both know it's true," I spat out and got up and went to my room.

Ok, so maybe I was a bit angry with my mother, a little over a year ago she pushed me into moving out with my then boyfriend, Christopher and it all went horribly wrong. I ended up in the hospital. I just kept on thinking that if she had left the decision up to me, I would have waited. I don't know if it all would have ended the same way – but I'd like to think it would have been different.

My inner critic kept telling me that I still could have followed my gut and just said 'no' to moving out with Christopher, and it was right, I guess it was just easier to blame someone else.

I was still brooding in my room when I heard a gentle knock on the door, it opened a crack and a hand slid in waving a white sock as a surrender flag. "Is it safe to come in?" David asked.

"Of course."

He walked in and sat down next to me on my bed, replacing his sock. "Your mums pretty upset you know."

"Yeah I know, I shouldn't have said anything to her – I just want her to stop talking about relationships with me. Why can't she just wait until I'm ready?"

"Well, number one she's always been like that, and number two, have you ever thought that she really does blame herself over what happened?"

I looked down, picking at an imaginary speck on my pants as I thought about this. "Maybe she does, but she behaves like she can't wait to have me married off and moved out again."

He put an arm around me and hugged me to him, "You know it's not like that, she loves you. I think she just wants the fairy tale for you."

We sat in silence for a while, me with my head rested on his shoulder and him with his arm still around me.

"Hey Trina?" David spoke, nudging me gently with his shoulder.

"Hmm?" I murmured.

"Do you blame me for what happened too?"

I sat bolt upright and looked at him, "No! How could I do that?"

"Because I couldn't protect you," he looked vulnerable with his eyes downcast. My heart ached with sorrow at the thought of him blaming himself.

"David, if anything, I am annoyed at myself for not listening to you when you said you didn't trust him. I stupidly thought it was just male bravado, and you would get used to each other. I didn't expect it all to explode the way it did, but it did. So now we move on," I said and squeezed his leg in reassurance.

He reached out and ran his finger over the still pink scar that ran down the side of my face along my hairline and past my ear. "Does he ever call you?"

"Yes," I whispered moving my hair to cover that side of my face. "But it's nothing to worry about - he just leaves messages; I haven't seen or spoken to him since you got me out of there... Listen, I have to go and talk to mum, I need to tell her I'm sorry for being a bitch." I stood up to leave and finish this conversation. Christopher wasn't a subject I liked to stay on for too long.

"Alright, I have to go and meet someone anyway."

"Of course you do; you man whore," I joked with him.

He smiled and kissed me on the cheek, "I'll see you later, be nice to your mum."

"I will."

David headed for the front door, calling out goodbye and thanks for dinner to my mother who was in the kitchen washing the dishes.

I walked over to her and put my head on her shoulder, "I'm sorry mum."

She stopped what she was doing and leaned against the sink sobbing, "You're right," she choked out.

"No I'm not."

She turned around to face me, "But it's true Katrina, if I hadn't encouraged you to move in with him when he asked, it never would have happened."

"You don't know that, it could have happened anyway. Mum, I'm sorry I said what I did – I don't blame you. I don't blame David. I only blame him. That's it. Mum, I just snapped because I don't want to talk about boys and dating right now. I've got enough on my plate as it is. I will date again when I'm ready, and I will do it on my terms ok?"

"Ok," she sniffed, "and please don't move out. I missed you when you were gone, and I'm glad to have you back."

I gave her a hug and grabbed a tea towel to dry the dishes. "Where did David go?" she asked.

"Oh off to meet his current girl for a quickie I think," I told her nonchalant.

"Katrina! Why do you have to be so crass?" she chided, flicking bubbles at me to make light of the situation.

I grabbed some and flicked back at her laughing. "Because I like seeing your face go all pink!"

The tension broken, we fell into easy conversation about

anything but relationships.

Chapter 5

I woke with a start the next morning way before my alarm was due to go off after a night filled with unsettling dreams. Giving up on sleep I decided to head to the pool for training early.

I flicked on my bedside lamp before I swung my feet out of bed, catching my reflection in the mirror – I was a mess; my blonde hair was sticking up all over the place, and I had a crust from drool at the corner of my mouth. My normally clear blue eyes were dull and bloodshot with dark circles underneath them, and my golden tan looked pale causing my scar to look an angry red instead of the pink it had begun to fade to.

I pulled out a baby wipe and cleaned my face, discarding it before I raked my hair back into a ponytail. I squeezed the cream I used to help fade my scar onto my finger and rubbed it in – it was getting better; you could barely notice it when I was wearing makeup, or if I had my hair out, I was lucky that was the only facial scar I got.

Sighing to myself, I quickly put on my bathers along with a pair of shorts and a hoodie jacket. I padded quietly into the kitchen and grabbed a banana as well as my training bag before I slipped out into the cool morning air.

I usually trained with a squad so the coach could help me with my stroke as swimming was my weakest leg but being there this early I would miss them. I hadn't even checked if I could come at that time, something I wished I had considered before driving there.

Thankfully, they let me in and after a quick chat with the coach; I was allowed to join the squad in the water. I spent two hours swimming up and down the pool trying to clear the fog out of my mind.

I had lied to David the night before, I had seen Christopher, he had come to the hospital after David had gotten me out of the flat, and I had promised not to press any charges, as long as he wasn't home when I went to collect my things.

He had broken down and cried, begging me not to leave him. If I hadn't been laying in a hospital bed, I might have changed my mind, but I wasn't interested in risking a repeat performance. I wasn't really sure that I could survive another one.

He kept sending gifts and would call me to beg me to take him back, and I did cave and meet him once for coffee, but it was just to say that I needed him to stop with the gifts and the begging, it was over. Now he only called occasionally to say he missed me.

I probably should have told someone that I saw him, but I feared that if David, Aaron or my father knew they would follow me and kill him.

Once I was too exhausted to think about my problems, I dragged myself out of the pool and went into the change rooms to shower before heading off to uni.

***

David met me on my way to the lecture rooms. "Hey babe! Did you sort everything out with your mum?"

"Yeah I did, thanks. What's with calling me 'babe'? Isn't that your generic name for the girls you date so you don't have to remember who you're with?" I teased as I elbowed him playfully in his side.

He reached his arm around my shoulders and hugged me to him good-humouredly. "I could never forget you Katrina – you're the sole reason I get up every morning," he told me solemnly.

"You're an idiot," I laughed. "Did you get all of your reading done?"

"Yes! And my eyes are burning from working so hard – seriously; it's a full-time job keeping up with them! I might have to take a speed-reading course or something."

"You know, if you didn't spend so much time at my place or going out with your girlfriends – you'd find it a lot easier."

"This is true my dear Trina, but the heart wants what the heart wants, and mine wants good company in the form of my best friend and good sex in the form of a willing but not too clingy partner."

"Eloquently put," I told him as we rounded the corner and entered the lecture room to take our seats, David turned around and started chatting up the girl sitting behind us, and I unpacked my things and turned my mobile phone to silent.

After the lecture we had a short break which we spent in the library – me studying, David socialising; he drove me mad with this as I worked so much harder than he did, and he's the one that got the better marks. Almost every assignment came back with a Distinction or High Distinction for him while I tended to get Credits with the occasional Distinction thrown in when I was lucky.

After the library, we parted ways as we both did double degrees. My other degree was Humanities and David's was Commerce, so this was an area where we both had to go solo.

"We still painting the town red after work tomorrow night?" he asked me before heading off.

"Absolutely, I want to go to check some of the bars out at Darling Harbour."

"Sounds like a plan, I'll pick you up from your work, and we'll walk down together."

"Cool, see you then."

"Bye Babe," he said mischievously.

"Har har har, go to class," I told him as I watched him walk away laughing to himself.

Chapter 6

It was Friday, and I was at work again; the conversation of the day was based around Friday drinks and where everyone was going afterwards. I told Kayley and Albina that I was going to stay for maybe half an hour and then go out with David to Darling Harbour.

"We're going to Pontoon," said Kayley. "You should come too."

"Who's David? Your boyfriend?" asked Albina.

"No he's just a friend," I directed at Albina, "and yes we might stop in to Pontoon," I said to Kayley.

I decided that after the altercation I had had with Bianca on Wednesday that I might actually go to the gym upstairs and do some weights instead of running again.

I had my bag over my shoulder and was waiting for the lift at lunch time when I saw Elliot walk around with his running gear on. He noted me with my work wear still on and gave me a questioning look.

Maybe half a dozen other people were waiting for the lift to go down and knowing he didn't like feeding gossip, I just pointed to my gym bag and indicated that I was going up. He nodded slightly in acknowledgement as the elevator pinged and the doors opened on its way down. Impatiently I pressed the up button again, when I stepped back I nearly stood on Elliot's foot.

I spun around startled and placed my hand on his rock-hard chest to steady myself; I had assumed he got on the lift with everyone else. "What are you still doing here? Couldn't you fit in the lift?" I asked confused, slowly forcing my hand to move back to my side instead of letting it caress the smooth skin that was showing at the neck of his singlet, like it wanted to.

"I thought I'd come up too, are you using the treadmills, the bikes? You're not doing a spin class or aerobics are you? Because I won't join you doing that."

"I'm doing weights," I informed him, taking a step back to gain some distance so I could breathe. I looked at him quizzically, wondering what his game was.

"Alright, weights it is," he agreed while watching the numbers of the elevators. "What?" he asked when he saw the way I was looking at him.

"When did this happen?" I said moving my finger to point between myself and him. He looked at me as if he didn't know what I was talking about. "Since when did we become training buddies? What happened to the Elliot, who doesn't like to be seen talking to any of the girls in the office?"

"Oh, I'm not Elliot, Elliot's my evil twin remember? I'm Evan."

I laughed, "Alright then Evan, as I recall, you're the friendly one – are you going to drinks tonight?"

"Elliot goes most weeks, but I could be persuaded to take his place. Will you be there?"

The elevator pinged and we both got on with a couple of other people who worked on the floors above us.

"I'm only going for maybe half an hour, then I'm going out with a friend."

"A friend huh? Would this friend be a guy friend or a girl friend?"

"A guy friend, a very platonic guy friend," I replied as the lift doors opened and we both stepped off and entered the gym.

Elliot was a member and had a card on his key chain that he scanned to get through the turn styles. I told him I needed to line up to pay for my visit.

He shook his head, "Wait there. I'll get you a guest pass."

I stood still for a couple of minutes while he spoke to a girl behind the counter who was smiling and batting her eyelashes at him more than was necessary for a business exchange, and who could blame her really? Elliot was divine to look at. He thanked her as she handed him the guest pass, and he walked towards me signalling that I come over to him. He scanned the piece of paper that was my pass, and the turn styles activated to let me through.

"Thank you for that. Looks like Evan is a bit of a flirt," I said noting the way the girl at the counter was all sweetness and light when he was looking but had nothing but death stares for me.

He looked over at her, and she smiled sweetly, "Just one of the perks of being the good twin," he joked.

"Doesn't Elliot flirt?"

"No, he doesn't know how to have fun; he's all about the work that guy."

I laughed and said that I was going to get a locker and change. He told me to come and find him on the treadmills when I was ready.

When I had finished I found him running full trot on a treadmill looking out the window where you could see people milling about below. I took my time walking up to him, so I could spend some time ogling him, I wasn't the only one who liked what I saw, there were quite a few women who had migrated toward the machines that surrounded him and were happily staring at his arse and his long muscular legs as he ran without falter like a well-oiled machine. With one last sinful look at his behind, I walked around to let him know I was there.

He smiled, "Do you want to warm up first?" he asked as he slowed to a walk.

I took great delight in the disappointed faces of the women around us as he got off and touched my shoulder before he gave me his machine. He stood in front of me stretching and watching me as I gradually picked my pace up to a run. I don't know if it was the way he was looking at me or the running, but I was starting to feel incredibly warm.

"Jesus Christ, you have better abs than I do!" he exclaimed.

I put my hand on my stomach; I was wearing a pair of short black running tights and a mint green crop top that had the running bare logo printed across the breast area, leaving my midriff exposed. Under his scrutiny, I suddenly felt like I was naked, my insides clenched, and I almost faltered my step, almost.

I smiled and dug out a bit of bravado saying, "Well, if I had known I was going to show you up, I would have covered up a little more." He laughed and continued stretching.

After watching him for a moment, I chewed my lip as I worked up the courage to say, "Show me your abs then."

He raised his eyebrows, and slowly complied. I think I held my breath as I watched, noticing that a couple of the women around us had craned their necks to have a look as well. I slowed the tread mill down and jumped off, walking closer to him and making a big show of inspecting him.

"Nothing wrong with them," I told him, my voice deeper and more breathy than I intended. I admired his six pack by running my fingertips over the ridges – they were much more defined than mine were, I could see the hint of that sexy V shape that men get peeking over the waist band of his shorts. I snatched my hand back as my insides clenched again, and I purposely squeezed my inner muscles to try to get control of my arousal.

He cleared his throat and lowered his shirt, "I cheated; I flexed them," he said.

I laughed, and my laugh sounded seductive too – what was going on with me? I stepped away again, gaining that much-needed distance between us and took a deep breath to calm myself before I spoke, "I saw that, but I wasn't going to say anything," I sounded much more normal that time.

"So uh… do you have a set weights routine, or do you just wing it?"

"Set routine," I said with my normal tone, producing the folded up piece of paper that I'd had tucked in the back zip pocket of my running tights.

He took it from me, ensuring that our hands connected when he did. The electricity between us shot up my arm and set me off again. Pelvic floor exercises weren't on that list, but I was definitely getting a lot in today.

He unfolded the paper perusing the list of exercises and took a step back from me. "You do cleans?" he asked.

"I do," I said taking the piece of paper back off him, not connecting this time. I spun on my heels and headed off to the first exercise on my list with Elliot trailing behind me.

We moved around the gym following my weights routine together. It was like a sweaty erotic dance between us - each time I looked at him, I had to restrain myself from jumping on top of him and running my tongue over those beautiful abs of his.

When we were finished, we both stood there shaking out our muscles before dropping to the ground to stretch a bit to cool down.

"So, I was watching you today," Elliot started. I raised my eyebrows suggestively; he smiled and went on, "I couldn't help but notice you've got some pretty decent scars – did you come off your push bike or something?" Elliot asked me.

I instinctively touched my arms. "No, not the bike; I wasn't training when it happened. I ah, actually went through a glass sliding door a while back." I went on quickly with the story I have told so many times recently, "I was lucky I put my arms up to protect my face, so I only got this one," I moved my hair to show him. He lifted his hand and touched the one on my shoulder, sending those sparks of electricity through my body again, curling my toes. I closed my eyes for a moment from the intimacy of his touch.

"And this one?" he softly traced the scar tissue along my shoulder, his voice deep and personal as he spoke. We locked eyes for a moment, and you could feel the shift in the air. Electricity was humming around us pulling us toward each other. I licked my lips as we drew closer. *Don't do this!* my common sense screamed.

I snapped my head back and let go of my hair so it fell away from my face providing a curtain. Shooting to my feet, I took a step away from him; I needed that distance between us. I needed us to stay in the friend zone.

I touched my shoulder, cleared my throat and answered him as if it hadn't seemed like he was about to kiss me, "Yeah that one too; I went through like this." I demonstrated the protective stance I was in when I went crashing through the window. Trying to bring us back to the easy banter we had enjoyed just moments before.

He looked down at the ground and seemed slightly wounded by my retreat, but he followed my lead and tried to continue the conversation, "So how did you manage to go through the window?"

I wasn't going to answer that one fully, that story turned me into a victim, and I wasn't willing to be put in that box. "Oh, just stupidity on my part," I told him as I picked up the paper with my routine on it, folded it and stuffed it into my pocket. "I'm going to hit the showers, see you back at the office, or at drinks maybe." I started heading off, "Oh and thanks again for the pass – I owe you one."

He just nodded at me and ran his hand through his sweat slicked hair. My chest felt full and heavy as I carefully breathed out on my way to the showers. What was going on here? I knew that I was attracted to him, and I could tell there was something there for him too, but I also knew we could both lose our jobs if we started seeing each other. I had thought he was safe because of that, I really didn't think he would do anything to risk it – maybe I was wrong.

Chapter 7

"You ready to head in?" Kayley called out to me from the doorway of the library.

I popped my head up to look at her over the partition, "Yep, just give me a sec to turn off my computer." Clicking it closed, I pushed myself away from my desk to walk with Kayley to my first Friday night drinks.

Kayley had changed from the skirt and blouse combination she had worn throughout the day to tight black pants, and a matching singlet top covered in sequins. She had tied her dirty blonde hair up into a messy ponytail and put on large gold hoop earrings, darker makeup and a pair of cute red kitten heels.

"You look nice! Are we supposed to dress up for this?" I asked her, looking down at my own outfit; I was wearing a pleated brown, purple and white tartan skirt with a white three quarter sleeved blouse and a purple sweater vest. I looked very dowdy in comparison.

"No you don't have to dress up; some of us just get changed to hit the clubs afterwards. You will be fine the way you are," she assured me. "Come on, let's go." She linked her arm in mine and guided me towards the conference room.

I paused in the doorway and surveyed the room as we entered, "I didn't expect quite so many people," I commented. There were maybe 30 people inside, there was a fairly good mix of support staff to solicitors and a couple of partners were in there too.

Music was playing at a reasonable level, and the bar was laden with bottles of wine and beer as well as a couple of spirits and soft drinks.

"Hi you made it!" Carl said as Kayley and I walked towards our now usual group.

I smiled gratefully, as he reached over to the bar and handed me a glass of white wine. Taking slow sips, I continued to look around the room to see who was in attendance. My heart fell a little when I couldn't see Elliot anywhere. I didn't think he was really going to talk to me here, but I wanted to see him, especially after our near kiss that afternoon. I felt that if he came, then our friendship was ok, but if he didn't, then he was annoyed with me.

"Taking it all in?" Mary said as she moved to stand next to me.

"Um, yeah," I said as brightly as I could. "This is the first time I have been to one of these things, so I didn't really know what to expect." I snuck a glance toward the door as it opened to see who entered.

To my disappointment, it was Bianca and Beth. They walked inside and instantly started working the room. I had to hand it to them – there were good. They spoke to all the solicitors as they passed them on their way to sit down and chat to the partners, each person looked pleased to chat with them. I guessed that Bianca saved her wrath only for those she saw as a threat somehow. If I didn't know any better, I could be mistaken for thinking she was a nice person after witnessing her here.

"So, what did I miss?" a male voice asked low and close to my ear.

"Who the hell let you in here?" I asked David, as I spun around, happily embracing him. I looked at my watch, "You're early!"

"I followed the sounds of frivolity when I got here, and

someone was kind enough not to check who was behind them when they keyed their code in the door."

"Very James Bond of you," I told him, impressed.

"And I'm here early because I didn't want to go to drinks at my work tonight," he leaned in close and said behind his hand, "let's say things are a little awkward right now between me and the girl I banged in the filing room last month."

I shook my head good naturedly and turned my attention back to Kayley and the others.

"Aren't you going to introduce us to your very attractive friend here?" asked Albina, giving David an approving once over. He smiled his 'yeah, I'm hot' smile and ran his fingers through his already messy hair to move it out of his eyes. I noticed Albina lick her lips seductively at him.

A humourless laugh escaped my lips; this always happens when other girls know that David, and I aren't together. I suddenly become their gateway to becoming a notch on David's bed post – the last time I checked I wasn't a pimp, so I gave a general introduction and excused myself to go and freshen up before I dragged David out of there to go and check out Darling Harbour.

As I left the conference room, my breath caught a little. Elliot was coming towards me. A smile crept over my lips but froze when I saw his eyes drift over my shoulder to check if anyone was looking.

"Are you leaving?" he asked looking at his watch. "I thought you were staying a while."

"Not just yet. I'm going to the bathroom to freshen up before I go out with my friend."

He looked nervously at the conference room again, "Ok. I might see you in there."

I nodded and went into the bathroom to reapply my makeup and brush my hair. I wished I had brought some clubbing clothes with me now too, but my work clothes would have to do for tonight.

I sighed as I looked at my reflection; I was good at making myself look casually pretty, but I was terrible at getting dressed up for nights out on the town - something my mother tried to coach me on, and I of course fought her on. Although I wished I'd listened a bit more now.

I returned to the conference room, a lump forming in my throat when I saw Bianca flicking her hair while talking to David, the last thing I needed was for David to do his usual hump and dash with someone I worked with – especially Bianca, I could only imagine how nasty she'd get if she felt used by him.

"Hey," I interrupted as cheerily as I could focusing on David, "You about ready to go?"

"Ah, yeah sure – but these guys are all heading off to Pontoon soon. You want to wait and go with them? It'll be fun with a big group."

"We'd love it if you came," Bianca cooed at me but touched David's arm.

"Oh, I don't…" I started to say before Kayley bounced over and excitedly told me that she was so happy I was going to Pontoon with them. I finished my sentence under my breath, "…think it was ever my decision. So why not."

"It'll be good for you," David murmured near my ear.

"Just keep your hands off the girls I work with," I warned him.

"Why? You jealous?" he challenged me.

"No, I just don't need you…"

"Hi, I'm Elliot," Elliot stuck his hand out in greeting towards

David, "you must be Katrina's *friend,*" was that jealousy I detected just then?

David took his hand and shook it firmly, "Hey man, I'm David and yes I'm Katrina's *best* friend." They stood there having one of those silent battles of the mind that males tend to have when they are sizing each other up.

"Ok," I interrupted the exchange, beginning to feel uncomfortable – especially with Bianca watching; what the hell was Elliot doing? "David, would you mind getting me another glass of wine?"

"Sure," he said moving off towards the bar, eyeing off Elliot.

"I'll come too," Bianca said trotting off to join him and leaving Elliot, and I standing together. The noise in the room was rising as everyone started to relax and become more animated with a couple of drinks in them.

"Hi," he smiled at me then cleared his throat and looked as though he just realised where he was and went into office mode. "How has your first week been?" he asked me politely.

Fine - I could play this game too, "Well *Elliot* my first week has been fine. I've met a lot of nice people, and my job is pretty easy. Excuse me," I said curtly and was about to turn and walk away, when he gently touched my arm to stop me.

"Wait," I turned around to look at him again. "It's probably none of my business but is that guy your boyfriend? You seem pretty close."

"Elliot, you're absolutely right – it is none of your business; but for future reference if I say someone is my friend that's exactly what they are."

Elliot nodded solemnly and then laughed at himself, "I'm sorry; I just don't know how to do this."

"Do what? Talk nicely to a girl twice in one day? Or behave like a person at work?"

"Both I guess, you know what's at risk here," he said quietly.

"Then why are you even standing here?" I asked him.

"I don't know, I guess I figure there's no harm in talking to the people – the person; I want to talk to."

"Well then perhaps you should get Evan out here. He seems to know how to have fun," I joked. He smiled and nodded slowly at me, looking at his hands. "You know, you can probably be seen hanging out with people from work and not cause too much of a stir. You're over thinking all this."

"What? I hang out with Andrew over there. That counts." I looked over to see another of the junior solicitors - a very tall lanky, dark-haired guy who looked around the same age as Elliot; standing in the corner speaking quietly with one of the account managers, she was a little more than half Andrew's height with brown curly hair and looked to be in her mid to late 20s.

I smiled and asked if maybe he and his friends would like to join us at Pontoon later. "And when I say you – I mean Evan," I grinned.

An amused smile crept over his face, "Alright. I'll think about it."

David returned with my drink, Bianca trailing behind him, and handed it to me. "Everything alright?" he asked giving Elliot the once over again.

"Everything's fine David," I assured him, touching his chest in a 'back down' gesture, "Why don't you get to know some of the guys here, instead of hitting on all the girls?" I moved over to Kayley, Albina and Jo to socialise were there wasn't so much tension.

We ended up staying there drinking until 8pm before we all headed off as a group to Pontoon at Darling harbour – Elliot included. As we walked he introduced me to his friend Andrew and the woman he had been talking to earlier, Carmen. It turns out that she lives near David and myself, so we made a plan to catch the train home together and swapped mobile numbers, in case we got separated.

Pontoon was packed. The music was loud, the air was thick with body heat and the bar was ten people deep - you needed to be slightly aggressive to maintain your position so you would actually get to the front of the line.

Bianca had David well within her sights and wouldn't leave his side. He offered to get me a drink, and she told him that she would love one too so he obliged, enjoying the attentions of such an attractive woman.

I wasn't very willing to engage Bianca in conversation, so I attempted to busy myself trying to spot where the rest of our group had gotten to. Elliot was talking to Andrew and Carmen, and Kayley and the others had gone straight for the dance floor. I smiled as I watched them swaying their hips with their arms above their heads getting plenty of attention from surrounding men.

Bianca obviously didn't mind talking to me though, "So, what are you? A cutter or something?" she sneered indicating my scarred forearms.

I was categorically taken aback this time – *who the hell says things like that?!* I searched her face to gain some sort of understanding but found myself expecting a forked tongue to flick out of her mouth.

"*What* is your problem?" I frowned at her.

"You're my problem, I can see the way you're going after Elliot."

"I'm not going after Elliot, I have to talk to him for work and we get along – that's all," I told her feeling incensed in her presence.

"Well keep it that way, Beth's been working on him for months, and she doesn't need some Amazon like you getting in the way. God only knows what he sees in you anyway - if you didn't wear skirts and have long hair, I would swear you were a boy."

I looked over at Elliot and saw that Beth had moved in and was chatting happily to him, Andrew and Carmen. They all looked neat and tidy together. He was smiling. She was smiling – I had to admit they looked good together. As I watched, I saw her link her arm with his and rest her head on his shoulder laughing. Jealousy flared within me as he laughed with her and put his arm around her, giving her a squeeze. I looked away quickly, knowing Bianca was watching me react.

"I thought there was a 'no dating' policy at work."

"There is, but no one is going to tell on them; Look at them, it's only a matter of time before he breaks. Do you see how they look at each other? They're perfect together," she insinuated close to my ear.

A horrible possessive feeling tightened my chest when I had no right to be feeling that way. Mentally, I shook my head to try to clear it away.

"Bianca, I'm really not interested in Elliot," I lied. "I just got out of a serious relationship, and I'm not looking to enter a new one right now."

"You know. I really don't think it matters. The way he has his arm around Beth right now - I'd be surprised if he lasts the night," she said to me with faked brightness, I frowned because her words didn't match her voice, until I realised that David was standing behind me. "Thank you, David! You're such a sweetheart!"

He had returned with our drinks, a black Russian for me, a Vodka Cruiser for Bianca and a schooner of beer for himself. I took my drink with a thanks and knocked it back in two gulps before filling my mouth with the ice left over and crunching down angrily. I needed to move away from Bianca before I said something I was going to regret.

"I'm going to dance," I yelled to David. He looked at me and signalled did I want him to dance too, but I shook my head and indicated that I was going to dance with Kayley. He nodded his understanding and turned his attention back to seducing Bianca. I rolled my eyes as I walked away, was there any woman off-limits to him?

Kayley's group had grown and she squealed, hugging me as I squeezed in next to her, she seemed pretty drunk at this point and was having a great time. She started to yell in my ear, so she could introduce me to the other people she was dancing with, they were mainly her house mates; all Irish - they came over to Australia on a working visa at the same time as she did. One guy was her cousin, and he leaned into me to shake hands and introduce himself properly. "I'm Connor," he yelled above the music in his Irish lilt.

I was obviously more tipsy than I realised as I actually blushed and giggled at him as I took his hand in greeting. I released his hand and settled into the music, closing my eyes and trying to forget about the men in my life and focus instead, on having a good time. Before I knew it Connor, and I had broken off from the group and were pressed up against each other rocking together to the music. He kept talking close to my ear, I couldn't really hear him but I was laughing anyway because his voice was really sexy and the heat, coupled with the alcohol were making me forget myself.

But, when he leant in to kiss me, I panicked. I pushed him away and wrestled my way through the crowd to get outside for some fresh air.

The moment I stepped out, I felt the cool air coming off the water wash over me, I gulped it in greedily and walked further out along the wharf to escape the noise as well. *What was wrong with me? That's not the kind of person I am, I don't dirty dance with random guys at bars.*

"Katrina?" I turned to the voice. My head started to throb as I realised Elliot had followed me out.

I looked over my shoulder at him and recognised that I was pissed off at him. "Go away Elliot," I told him sternly.

"No, I'm not going away. What the hell was that about? You invited me out, to what? Watch you dry hump some guy on the dance floor?"

I spun around, "What? You haven't even spoken to me since we got here. Instead you've been focused on Beth!" I shook my head and stepped away from him. "Oh my god, what am I even doing? I've spoken to you what? Three, four times? We've trained together twice. I don't even want a relationship right now, and I'm acting like some jealous girlfriend. Fuck me!" I complained as I ran my hands over my head in frustration. Having him around me was making me act stupid.

"No, it's not just you. I'm behaving the same way - from the moment I met you, I've done nothing but break my rules to spend time with you," Elliot said gently as he moved closer to me. "In a week you've got me at a bar chasing you out because I felt insanely jealous watching with that guy, and I acted like a fool at work when I saw you with David. I just... I can't stop thinking about you Katrina. I don't even think I care anymore if we're not supposed to date because of work – all I know is that I want you, and I don't want you to be with anyone else."

"You could lose your job over this Elliot!"

"So could you," he said moving even closer to me.

"Who cares about my job, it's entry level - I can easily get another one," his hand slid up and caressed the side of my face causing a rush of longing to course through my body. I leaned into his touch and closed my eyes as that magnetic attraction between us started to pull us closer together, despite my own resistance.

"I care about your job. My days are better when you're in them," he whispered as he drew my face towards his and ever so lightly, brushed his lips against mine. I let out a slight whimper as he circled his arms around me. I felt myself melt into him, a merging of bodies unlike anything I'd ever felt before. I parted my lips as his tongue started to tease me, searching my mouth for a response and sucking my lips into his. My reaction became urgent as I reached my arms behind his head and entwined my fingers into his hair, pressing myself against him.

His hands moved down towards my buttocks, lifting me up in a show of strength as if I weighed nothing. I circled my legs around his waist, clinging to him and kissing him like I was an addict, and he was my drug, not giving a thought to where we were.

My emotions were swimming around in my head as I gave into my need for this man's touch. I tightened my own grip around him as my tongue dove into his mouth more forcefully, exploring him, drinking him in.

"Um Katrina?" an Irish accent broke the moment.

My eyes popped open, and I pulled away from Elliot slowly. Peering over his shoulder, I saw Connor standing there with a look of disbelief on his face, closely followed by Kayley, David and worst of all Bianca. She stood there behind the others shaking her head disapprovingly, while I stayed frozen - my hair a mess, my lips swollen from kissing Elliot so hard, and my legs still wrapped around his waist.

"What's going on?" he whispered to me not daring to turn around.

I pushed myself away from him and lowered my legs while he supported my weight until my feet were on the ground.

Embarrassed from losing control in such a public place I looked from Elliot to the group of people watching and stammered out, "I…I'm sorry. I have to go." I dashed off through Darling Park with the single thought of making it to Town Hall station, so I could go home.

I heard David yell, "No! I'll go!" He came after me at a run and caught up to me before I had even exited the concrete park.

"Trina!" he called out as he caught up. "What was that about? Are you ok?"

"No, I'm not ok. I'm an idiot! I just made an absolute fool of myself," I whined continuing to walk top speed.

"Katrina, slow down," David pleaded with his hand on my shoulder, "Talk to me properly."

I stopped and looked at him face on, "I don't know what I'm doing David!" Tears of frustration fell from my eyes. "Every time I'm around him, I can't think straight. I find myself flirting and being completely unable to control myself."

"Hey baby girl, don't cry. Everything will be alright," David cupped my face with his hands and wiped his thumb across my cheek to dry my tears away.

"I don't even feel capable of having a relationship right now – I don't want this David! - Not to mention the fact that I have Bianca gunning for me, and it's only been a week! This is all way too fast and way too much drama – this isn't me! This isn't the kind of person I am!" I explained lifting my hands in vexation.

"Bianca? What's she got to do with it?"

"Bianca is nothing but a bitch towards me, David. She might have been all gorgeous sex kitten towards you tonight, but as soon as you left me with her at the bar she asked me if I was a cutter because of my scars and then warned me off Elliot. Every time I see her, she has something bitchy to say to me – she keeps calling me a boy! I can't believe that of all the girls in my office, you had to choose her to hang around tonight."

David took a step back, his brows knitted tightly together. "You never told me she was giving you a hard time. You hardly talk about your work at all! All I know is its easy work, and the people are nice. I only know you like Elliot because I caught you staring after him on your first day with this infatuated look on your face; otherwise I'd have no clue. You have to talk to me Katrina. We're best friends, and before Christopher came along and fucked everything up you did tell me everything, don't push me away too ok?" he told me earnestly. He stared into my eyes to show me how serious he was and then drew me into a hug. I sighed against his shoulder, realising I hadn't been a very good friend lately. I promised that I would talk to him more about what was going on with me.

As soon as I had calmed down, we walked arm in arm towards the train station, remembering half way there that we were supposed to catch the train back with Carmen.

Feeling guilty I stopped to call her and tell her where we were. She asked for us to wait for her to catch up, so we stood and chatted while we paused.

"I wasn't going to do anything with Bianca," he said during a quiet moment. "Well, not tonight anyway," he added with that lopsided grin of his.

I couldn't help but smile back, "It doesn't matter David. You can sleep with whoever you like. I just sort of panicked about Bianca tonight - because I'm pretty sure she might be a siren and would eat you if you got too close," I told him, trying to lighten up the mood a bit.

He laughed a little through his nose, but stayed fairly serious. "So are you going to tell me what's been going on with Elliot?"

I took a deep breath, not really wanting to share, but I told him about how we had been training together and that there were a couple of charged moments between us when we did. I then told him how I had been confused because of how Elliot was running so hot and cold whenever we were near people from the office.

As I finished David looked over my shoulder and lifted his head upwards to tell me someone was approaching. I turned around and saw Carmen walking towards us with both Andrew and Elliot.

"Hi!" she said brightly. "Thanks for waiting for me, I hate catching the train home by myself this late at night, I normally go home much earlier than this." Elliot stood beside her watching me intently, his eyes dark and serious.

"No worries," I said to her trying to mirror her smile as I tried to ignore Elliot's gaze as it bore through me. "Do you need a ride home at all? My car is at the station."

"Will you be sober enough to drive home?" asked Andrew.

"I'll be fine," I assured him, "I only had a few drinks. It takes an hour and a half to get home at this time of night so I'll be well and truly sober by then."

"I'd love a ride home, thanks," Carmen accepted, reaching up to Andrew and giving him a quick kiss goodbye. I watched the exchange and realised that Albina was right, the 'no dating' rule doesn't really stop anyone at all. However, it could definitely cause problems if the wrong people knew about you.

Elliot touched my hand and lifted it toward him a little, "Can we talk before you go?"

I nodded and squeezed David's arm to reassure him that I

was fine before walking a few steps away to talk to Elliot more privately.

"Listen about tonight, I'm sorry if I pushed you or embarrassed you in any way."

"You didn't Elliot, I embarrassed myself."

He studied my face for a moment, gauging my state of mind, before he continued, "Listen, about Beth – there's nothing going on with her, there never has been. I was only talking to her because she's my PA. I know she has a thing for me, but I try not to encourage it. Putting my arm around her tonight was… a lapse in judgement," he ran his fingers though his hair causing it to stick up at odd an angle, I curled my hands into fists as I resisted the urge to reach up and smooth it down for him. He frowned in thought and continued, "She was flirting with me, and I didn't want to be a jerk and just ignore her – so I tried to be friendly – but not too friendly," he shook his head and frowned again. "Obviously that's not what it looked like though… Listen, I spend time with you because I'm interested in you – I'm not interested in her; or anyone else." He reached out and brushed the backs of his fingers along my cheek, and I once again closed my eyes as his touch sent pleasure ripples through my body. "I hated seeing you dance with that guy tonight," he whispered as he stepped closer to me.

My head was clouded by his proximity, and I was finding it hard to breathe, let alone speak. I floundered for my words, "I... I don't know if I am ready for this Elliot. I don't know if I can do this. It's all too fast."

"Then we'll take it as slow as you want. Because, I don't think I could stay away from you, even if I wanted to," he pulled me closer to him and my breath caught as he leaned down and kissed me slowly. I felt like jelly in his arms as I relaxed against the hard plains of his body, languishing in the feeling of his mouth on mine. Out of breath, I felt as though I was trembling as we pulled apart from each other.

"Give me your phone," he released me and held out his hand. I fumbled through my bag and handed it to him, watching as he tapped in his number and called his own phone. "There, now we both have each other's numbers," he told me, as he handed me back my phone. I looked at my call list and noticed he saved it under 'Evan' and smiled to myself.

"We ready? There will be a train soon," called out David impatiently.

"Ok, we're coming," I told him. We all walked together toward Town Hall Station. Elliot took my hand and interlaced our fingers leaning in close to me. Carmen and Andrew held hands as well; David was the odd man out walking beside me with his hands in his pockets, and his head down. He had become very quiet, and I was worried about him.

Upon reaching the station we saw that the train was due in within a minute. David, Carmen and I said a quick good bye, rushed down the stairs to the platform as the train was pulling in and walked straight on board.

There were plenty of seats at that time of the night, so we settled in at the front of the carriage where we could face each other and chat on the way home. I spoke to Carmen, about how long she had been dating Andrew. She told me that they had been together for nearly a year. I was surprised that there hadn't been any repercussions at work for them.

"The no dating policy only becomes a problem if someone else has a problem with you dating. No one cares if Andrew and I are together. We keep to ourselves. Let's face it, he's no Elliot, so no one really takes any notice of us. You on the other hand, will have to be very careful, especially after tonight. A lot of girls really like Elliot and they are all going to have their noses out of joint when they find out he likes you. He normally doesn't give any of the girls the time of day, so you kissing him in public after only a week, is going to ruffle some serious feathers."

I leant back in the seat and let out a heavy sigh, "I know. We're going to have to hide it."

David sat forward frowning, "Listen, this may not be any of my business here but do you think that's wise? I'm all for you moving on, but I don't know if a secret relationship is a good thing for you Katrina," he pointed out haughtily.

"No David, I don't think it's wise," I sighed again and looked out the window at the passing lights of the tunnel, "but I can't stop thinking about him – I feel drawn to him, and I need to find out where that takes us; without either of us losing our jobs."

"I just want you to think about this seriously Trina. Before you were saying you didn't want a relationship, and that it was all happening too fast. Now you're talking about risking your job for a guy you've only known a week – You're flip flopping," he crossed his arms over his chest and put his feet on the seat across from him, doing exactly what the sign above his head told him not to do.

"I know what I'm doing David," I assured him.

"Well, I'm glad you know," he mumbled as he chewed on his thumb nail and stared out the window. I watched him for a moment as he only chewed his nails when he was agitated about something. He turned and met my eyes, and I knew from his look that then wasn't the time to talk to him.

Instead, I turned to Carmen, and we talked easily the rest of the way home with David only entering the conversation occasionally when Carmen asked him a direct question.

When the train pulled into Penrith Station David walked us both over the bridge and to my car.

"Will you come over tomorrow?" I asked him before he left.

He leaned forward and kissed me roughly on the cheek, "Sure," he said and raised his hand to say goodbye to Carmen. "It was nice to meet you," he told her.

"You too," she said quietly. "Is there something going on between you two?" she asked as she got into the car, "I mean, did you use to date or something?"

I started the car as soon as I saw David get inside his own. "No. We have never dated and there is nothing going on. He's just … protective of me; we've been through a lot together... as friends."

The explanation placated her, so she didn't ask any more questions, instead making small talk as she directed me towards her house. She thanked me for the lift as she got out of the car.

"You're more than welcome," I replied, "It was nice to get to know you tonight."

"Same to you and good luck with Elliot - it's nice to see him smiling," she said as she shut the door and waved to me before walking up the path that led to her door.

I watched until I saw her step inside her house. I put the car into drive and said to myself, "Luck huh? I think I'm going to need it."

Chapter 8

"Katrina! Wake up!" my mother called as she shook me from my sleep. Startled, I looked at her worried that something terrible had happened. "You were moaning and whimpering in your sleep! I could hear you from the kitchen," she told me, her face was full of concern. "It sounded like you were having a nightmare."

Pieces of the dream came floating back to me and the throbbing between legs told me that my dream wasn't scary at all. I sat up awkwardly and cleared my throat, "Mum, I'm fine… I don't even remember what it was."

"Oh look at you, you're all flushed," she attempted to reach out and smooth my hair like she always had when she thought I was upset. Moving my head to the side, I caught her hand and patted it reassuringly.

"Seriously mum I'm fine… thanks for worrying about me though."

"Ok, well – as long as you're sure....I'll let you get dressed then," she offered as she stood up and backed out of the room, "I was thinking of making eggs, do you want some or are you training first?"

"I'll train first," she nodded and shut my door on her way out.

I put my hands to my head as I lay back down on my bed remembering the dream I was having. I could see it clearly now - Elliot was settled in between my thighs lapping away like a pro; it felt incredibly real! *I can't believe I was moaning so loud my mother heard me!*

My face felt like it was on fire from both the dream and the embarrassment - I would have to remember to lock my door in the future.

I shifted a little in my bed. My clit was aching badly from the effects of the dream, it seemed a shame to waste such intense arousal – I bit my lip in daring, feeling pretty safe that my mother wasn't going to return any time soon, and decided to finish what my dream had started.

Closing my eyes, I slid my hand inside my pyjama bottoms and into my panties. I was so aroused that my body flinched involuntarily as my finger touched my sensitive spot and made its way between my sleek wet folds. I let out a silent moan as I reached two fingers inside and massaged my inner walls allowing the palm of my hand to press against my engorged clit. Sheathed in my wetness, my fingers moved like they were gliding over silk as I gently teased my own nub. Exploding in seconds, my core shattered into a million pieces, floating around me euphorically.

Afterward, I lay there breathing for a moment, my clit pulsing beneath my finger, thinking of nothing but him.

***

Grabbing an apple to eat before I started training I went and hitched my bike up to the back of my car. I wanted to go and visit Penrith lakes and ride around there for a couple of hours.

"Hey, where you going?" David asked as he walked up behind me, "I thought you wanted me to come around?"

"I did but I wasn't expecting you so early," I told him glancing at my watch. "It's eight fifteen; you're never out of bed at this time on a Saturday."

"I've got a lot on my mind," he said looking at his feet as he scuffed them on the driveway.

"Why don't you come for a ride with me, that way we can talk,"

I offered, wanting to clear the air between us.

"Sure, I'll just run home and change. Meet me there?" I nodded as he trotted off.

David only lived a couple of streets away from me. It was part of the reason we became such good friends during school. We lived at the far end of the bus route to school, so we got used to talking to each other and eventually started hanging out more often until we were inseparable.

I finished hooking up my push bike and went inside to get my helmet and bag. Dropping them onto the back seat, I got in my car and drove around to David's house. He had opened his garage knowing that I would load his bike for him while he changed.

I was tightening the bolt on the bike rack when he emerged from his house carrying his helmet and a water bottle. He walked over to the garage and pulled the door down before we got into the car and drove out to the Lakes.

We didn't really speak on the way. We just listened to the cd playing – he drummed his fingers to the beat, and I sang along to Lana Del Ray's *Off to the Races*. I snuck a glance at him every now and then, but I knew him well enough to know that he would talk to me when he was ready.

We got our bikes sorted out as soon as we arrived, and set off along the path to lap the lake for the next two hours. There were a few rowers training on the water and a coach cycling up and down the far side giving them instructions through a mega phone. I didn't speak, preferring to enjoy the scenery while I waited for David to get things straight in his head. That took almost half an hour.

"I wanted to talk to you about this thing you have with Elliot," he ventured.

"Alright, talk away."

"I just… can we stop for a minute?" he stopped his bike not waiting for an answer, and I followed suit. We both unclipped our shoes and wheeled our bikes off the track and sat down on the ground. He sat with his knees up as he pulled at the grass between his feet, breaking the blades up and letting them fall as he stared out at the water. "Are you sure having a secret relationship is a good thing?"

"It's not really that much of a secret - you know about it, and Carmen and Andrew know about it – so does half the office now, after witnessing us outside Pontoon; but we can play that off as drunken stupidity, I guess..." I let my words hang in the air as I focused on boats rowing past us and turned to watch their coach cycle past.

He let out a heavy sigh, "I'm just worried about you. I mean, how much do you really know about this guy?"

"I know that we get along really well, and that we're attracted to each other... I just... I don't know; I feel connected to him. Which is strange for me because I didn't think I'd want anyone for a long time, especially after Christopher."

"Well that's what I'm worried about"

"What that he's like Christopher?"

"Yes, and that if you go out with him in secret, then I'm not going to know where you are to get you out this time." He looked at me intently, and I could see the pain from the memories of that night in his eyes. "I don't know what I'd do if something like that happened to you again," he took my hand and turned it in his lap tracing his fingers over my scars, speaking to me softly. "What if something like this happens? What if you're not so lucky next time?... I'm happy that you've found someone Trina, but this secrecy thing doesn't sit right with me and seeing you with him last night, well – it just all felt wrong to me."

I took my arm back and squeezed his arm as I stood up, "I'll tell you what, every time I go somewhere with him I will text you so you know where I am. Is that fair?"

"What if I asked you not to see him?"

"You'd really ask that of me? It's been six months since I even looked at a guy, maybe that's too soon. I don't know - but I can't help how I feel right now. He's nothing like Christopher was."

He stood up and picked up his bike, "Alright, fine Katina, do whatever you want. But I'm not going to be the third wheel in your relationship this time ok? I'm not going to fight some guy so I can spend time with my best friend, I'm done with that." I looked at him and nodded imperceptibly, feeling a little stung by his words.

He faced his bike in the opposite direction to mine, and I frowned in question, "I'm going to ride home, are you ok on your own?"

"I'll be fine David, are you ok though? Are we ok?"

"I and we are fine Trina, I just worry is all. I'll see you later," he said sounding annoyed despite his words. He pushed off and headed home, not bothering to wave or to even look at me.

I watched him until I couldn't see him anymore. I understood that he was worried for me - the night he took me away from Christopher must have scared the shit out of him. I didn't remember much beyond the glass smashing and flashes of David carrying me and driving me to the hospital, but he remembers it all, and from what I could tell, it still haunted him that he couldn't do anything to stop it. Short of never dating again, I didn't know what would make him feel better.

***

Back at home I showered and had a late breakfast. My mum and dad had gone out shopping together, their favourite Saturday activity and my brother was once again with his new girlfriend – so I had the place to myself.

I hate to admit this, but I had my mobile phone sitting on the counter next to me waiting for it to ring. I sent a text to David to make sure it was working. **Thx 4 coming 2day, u got a date 2nite?**

A few seconds later I got a reply. **It's a secret.** I huffed out my breath and shook my head, he'd get over it all soon enough. I knew I was doing the right thing about Elliot, it's better to test the waters slowly and quietly before making a big deal out of everything. For now, I was just happy spending time with him.

I was getting antsy waiting on the phone, so I did a load of washing, cleaned my room, vacuumed the house and then hung the washing out. When I came back inside I noticed my phone was flashing at me, I rushed over to it like an excited school girl and looked at the missed call – Evan – about five minutes ago. No voicemail.

I took a deep breath and called him back. He picked up almost immediately, "Hey beautiful, I thought you'd have your phone on you."

"I was just outside being the dutiful daughter. What are you up to today?" from there it turned into one of those early relationship conversations where everything is interesting as long as you are connected somehow. We talked for almost an hour and when we disconnected, I couldn't wipe the goofy grin from my face.

Chapter 9

On Monday morning, when I arrived at work, I noticed Bianca sitting behind the reception desk eyeing me off smugly as I passed her by. I chose to take the high road for a change and smiled brightly wishing her a good morning. Although, every fibre of my being wanted me to shoot lasers at her from my eyes.

The moment I reached the library, Kayley raced over and followed me to my desk saying, "Oh my god, oh my god! I can't believe you kissed Elliot on Friday night! You my dear friend, are my new hero… Although I have to say you did upset my cousin by rushing off like that, but I will forgive you if you give me all the details." She grabbed one of the library chairs and wheeled it over to sit next to my desk looking at me expectantly.

I wasn't really sure what to tell her. I thought I could trust her, but I didn't know her well enough yet to give her information that could cost both myself and Elliot our jobs. So I decided on, "Kayley, I was pretty drunk on Friday, I don't actually remember much."

"What?!" she scrunched up and her face and sat back in her chair. "Are you telling me that you get the glorious Elliot Roberts to lock lips with you after only being here a week, and that's all you have to say about it? That's bullshit you don't remember - tell me it was hot, it was, wasn't it? I promise not to breathe a word!" she vowed with her hand on her heart and a solemn expression on her face.

I sighed, looking around to make sure no one was within earshot before I conceded. "Ok Kayley, it *was* hot, more than hot it was positively sizzling." That small admittance caused her to squeal and bounce on her chair happily.

"Please tell me you are dating him now, someone in this place has to and I would just love to have seen the look on Beth's face when Bianca told her."

"Sorry but no - I'm not dating him; it was a mistake Kayley and it can't happen again."

Kayley raised her eyebrows and nodded thoughtfully as she got up to move her chair back in place, "I don't believe you by the way."

"What do you mean?"

"That wasn't a mistake Katrina, look at you; you're beautiful, tall and into sports – same as him. The way I see it - it was bound to happen." She turned and walked out the door going back to her desk.

I was so busy watching Kayley that I didn't notice Priya come in after her. "Katrina, can I see you in my office please?" she asked me, looking unimpressed.

Anxiousness filled my head and buzzed in my ears. I nodded at her and looked out the window towards Kayley, who pulled her lip to the side in a grimace as she looked from Priya to me.

I immediately got up and followed Priya out, trying to walk tall and confidant despite feeling much like a head of cattle being led to slaughter. When we arrived at her office, Elliot was already sitting there with his legs crossed ankle to knee, his elbows on the chair arms and his fingers steepled.

I thought I saw a flicker of a smile pass his lips when he saw me, although he set his face to impassive as he watched us walk in and take the other two seats in the room. Seeing him there, I knew that Bianca had ratted us out.

Priya took her seat and leaned forward with her elbows on the desk to begin. "I got an interesting email this morning that said a few of your colleagues witnessed a rather public display of affection between you two." She eyed us both closely, "Is this true?"

Elliot and I looked at each other then turned back to her and shook our heads saying 'no'.

"So you're saying that if I ask around the office no one will have seen anything?"

"You could ask," said Elliot quickly, before I had managed to come up with an answer, "but who could really know what they saw. I admit I was seen kissing a woman on the wharf on Friday night, but no one could say for sure that it was Katrina. The woman I was with ran off embarrassed when a few of the staff from here called out to us from at least 50 metres away. So you see, they couldn't have really seen her properly – not from that distance."

"Is this true Katrina?" she asked looking at me suspiciously. I simply nodded in agreement not trusting myself to speak.

"I admit that I am friends with Katrina, we have similar sporting interests, and I admit to going running with her and to the gym. However, from what she tells me, she is already seeing someone called Evan, and that's not me is it Priya?"

"Evan huh?" she directed towards me; I nodded again, and she narrowed her eyes. "Alright then, I guess this meeting is over. I can't do anything without proof and there's no policy against you being friends so you're both free to go. But just let me remind you that if you are caught dating within the office one or both of you will lose your positions here."

"We understand. Thank you Priya for reminding us," said Elliot as he stood to leave.

"Yes, thank you Priya," I echoed as we both left and returned separately to our respective desks.

For the second-time today Kayley came rushing in for some gossip from me, "What did she want? Was Elliot in there with you?"

I didn't bother lying to her, "I think Bianca dobbed us in for Friday night."

"Oh no, are you in trouble?"

"No, we denied everything. Elliot said that whoever saw us was mistaken, and that he was kissing someone else. So she just reminded us of the policy and let us go."

"You'll have to be more careful then in the future."

I caught myself before I nodded and said, "There won't be an 'in future' Kayley. We're friends. That's all."

She pouted at me and scuffed her feet dramatically all the way out of the library and back to her desk.

My phone beeped in my bag, the screen told me that I had a new text from 'Evan', **Meet me for drinks after work?**

I smiled and typed back, **Not tonight, have training. How about Wed?**

The reply was almost immediate, **OK, will let u know where**

I placed my phone inside my top drawer and tried to focus on my work. Instead images from that erotic dream kept flashing through my mind.

***

When I arrived at work on Wednesday morning, I couldn't help but smirk when I saw Bianca's surprised face. She probably expected that I would have been fired for what happened with Elliot on Friday night.

I had kept to myself on Monday after leaving Priya's office, preferring to take my morning tea break at my desk, so I could avoid any questions. I missed them all again at lunch as I met up with David again. He was still behaving a bit off so I kept the conversation steered away from Elliot.

Tuesday was spent studying with David, as our uni exams were coming up soon. Spending time together was really helping to ease the tension between us; that was until Elliot called me at lunch time. I took the call in another room and kept the conversation brief, but David's demeanour had changed when I returned, and the study session ended very soon after.

I had hoped that by Wednesday, the interest at work in Elliot's and my relationship status had died down enough not to cause me any drama. I was about to find out as I ventured out of the library to take the new law magazine, and some sorted microfiche to Elliot.

I walked confidently over to his office determined to behave as professionally as possible. Waiving 'hi' to Beth, I showed her that I was just taking some things into Elliot's office. She nodded at me but didn't smile in return.

His door open, I tapped on the door frame and waited for him to notice me. Elliot was seated behind his desk, talking on the phone. During a pause in his side of the conversation he smiled, mouthing 'hi' and gesturing me inside. I marvelled that a simple smile from him could send my stomach excitedly flipping around inside my body.

I held up the items I had brought to him, and he pointed to his 'in' tray. I placed them there, and Elliot held up his hand signalling for me to wait while he continued talking and scribbled something down on a post-it note for me. *Star City Sports Bar 6:30pm?* I nodded before folding it and tucking it inside my pocket.

As I walked back Carl was wheeling a heavily laden filing trolley down the hallway, "Hey!" he said brightly when he saw me.

"Hi Carl," I smiled and stopped next to him.

"Well aren't you the topic of the week? I was inside on Friday night so I missed the show. I heard it was hot though," he said, winking at me.

I flushed a little and had to stop a smile from curling up the side of my lips, "I don't know what you're talking about Carl."

"Hmm, that's what they all say. Just watch yourself, ok. I've been privy to some pretty bitchy conversations – I don't think the other girls are taking it very well," he said the last part in a low exaggerated voice behind his hand.

I smiled and placed a friendly hand on his arm, "Thanks for letting me know."

I patted him on the back and returned to my desk where my internal line was ringing. "Hello Library, Katrina speaking."

"Hey, sorry I was on the phone," Elliot's baritone rumbled through the line caressing me places it shouldn't be over the phone.

"Don't sweat it, we can't talk here anyway. I think we're being watched fairly closely right now."

"Probably…You look hot today by the way," he whispered into the receiver.

I blushed and lowered my voice to a murmur, "Thank you. You're not so bad yourself."

I could practically hear him smiling, "Are you running today?"

"I am - I'll meet you there?"

"Sure, same place as last time."

We disconnected, and I worked through until morning tea time. I have to admit that after talking to Carl, I was nervous about facing everyone.

When I entered the break room, there were a few murmurs and stares as I lined up to get my coffee. I nodded hi to Kayley, who was already seated and smiling at me as I walked over with my drink in hand. Bianca took the opportunity to blatantly knock into me, spilling my coffee on my skirt. I bit back a retort, choosing to ignore her behaviour as I grabbed some paper towel and cleaned myself as best as I could. I was thankful that I'd had the foresight to wear dark colours.

I sat down with Kayley, Albina and Anne. "Wow, I feel like I'm back at high school," I laughed uneasily.

Albina raised her eyebrows and said to me, "Well you are public enemy number one at the moment. Bianca, and Beth are on a rampage."

Anne leaned in to talk quietly, "You should have heard Bianca yesterday. She was telling everyone that she got you fired."

"Well as you can see she didn't," I said. "Listen, nothing's going on and there's nothing to talk about, Biancas obviously trying to cause problems."

"Kayley and Connor saw you too, so don't deny it," added Albina.

"You know what, I was drinking. I don't really know what I saw," said Kayley.

I smiled gratefully at her and sighed, "I don't know why everyone's making a big deal out of it. I have known the guy for a week."

"Yeah and in that week you dry humped him on a wharf," said Albina.

I really didn't think that anything I said was going to convince them there was nothing between Elliot and I, so I stood to take what was left of my coffee to my desk instead. As I was leaving, I overheard Bianca saying, "Maybe he's into boys, and that's why." I spun around to give Bianca a piece of my mind as the others she was sitting with sniggered at her comment. I opened my mouth to speak, but she got there first, "Are you going to go and cut yourself now?"

The hatred I felt for her at that moment could be heard crackling through the air – in my mind, I was pouncing on her like an animal, clawing at her face and pulling out her hair; but in reality, I shut my mouth and spun on my heel not gullible enough to start something in front of everyone.

My face burned hot with humiliation as I put a call through to Elliot, he picked up on the second ring. "Elliot Roberts."

"Hey, it's me."

"Hey you, what's up?"

"I really don't think we should train together."

"What? Why?"

"Everyone in the break room was on my back about Friday. I think it would be a mistake to be seen together anywhere."

"Are you backing out on me?"

I sighed, not really knowing what I was doing, "I don't know, can we just cool it for a bit please? I have all this animosity directed at me right now, and I need to take a step back."

He was silent for a moment, "For how long?"

"I don't know, a week - or until this all dies down? I just … can we cool it for now, please?" I pleaded.

I could hear him sigh as his chair creaked over the phone. I imagined that he was leaning back running his hand through his hair. "Fine. I have to go," he disconnected.

I looked at the phone with a pain in my chest as I debated whether I was making the right decision by pulling back.

***

"I think you're making the right decision," David said at lunch. I had decided to skip my run altogether and called him to meet me at the food court in Sydney Tower instead. "Maybe get to know the guy a little more before you enter some kind of secret relationship with him. If he's that into you, then he'll wait til you're more comfortable to move forward."

"I just felt awful being the subject of office gossip and that Bianca; I know I get along better with guys but I don't think I have ever hated another girl until now."

"Maybe she just needs a good hard screw to make her happy? I could do that for you Trina, I could take the fall on that one – she may be a bitch but she's hot."

"And probably a bunny boiler! Do you really want that in your life?"

"If it takes her focus off you," he shrugged.

"Are you serious? You actually like her?" I was a little taken aback.

"Relax Trina, I'm just ribbing you. I'm not going to touch her. Although, maybe you should look for another job?"

"No, I don't want another job - Turner, Barlow & Smith is a great law firm. I'd rather stick it out and become a partner there so I can squash all my enemies like bugs!" I mashed my hands together to add emphasis to my words, as David watched with amusement playing on his lips.

Picking up my drink, I took a thoughtful sip. "I'm just going to take morning tea to my desk from now on. I need to avoid socialising," I decided.

"That's no fun! I was going to crash your drinks again this Friday."

"Not this week I'm afraid, I just want to lay low for a while."

"Alright, well do you want to grab some dinner and go out afterwards we can go clubbing if you want and I promise not to pick up any girls while we're out."

"That'll be a challenge, but it sounds good," checking the time on my watch, I stood up. "I need to get back to work." I told him as I lifted my tray to empty it into the nearest bin.

David followed suit, "Yeah me too, back to the ole grind hey," he leaned toward me and kissed my cheek goodbye, "I'll see you at the library to study tomorrow?" I nodded, "And don't worry about the shit at work. It'll all blow over. Someone else will get caught making out before you know it." He gave me a cheeky grin and winked, lifting his hand in a wave as he walked away.

Elliot was waiting for the lift when I returned from lunch, he had obviously returned from his workout as he was in his running gear, and his hair was wet with sweat.

"Hey," I said moving to stand next to him. "How was your run?"

"A little quiet," he said with a half-smile and down cast eyes.

I looked around and couldn't see anyone that I knew from our office in the group waiting or walking in the lobby, so I inclined my head towards the door leading to the stairwell.

"You want to walk with me?"

He nodded and walked over to hold the door open for me to walk through. I noticed him having one last look around before he followed me in.

We ascended the first two flights in silence before I began to talk. "Listen. I know I kind of freaked out today, but you have to understand how I'm being treated right now. It's like they think I've come in and cast some spell to steal another girl's boyfriend or something. You know? Like I purposely chose the guy they have been crushing on and cut their grass... Am I making sense?" I stopped on the landing and turned to face him.

"You are - but they aren't. I have been working here for a couple of years now, and I don't think I have given any of them reason to think I was interested in them. I've always kept my distance," he explained with his hands on his hips.

"Well we have to keep it that way for now, at least until all of this gossip dies down. It's not affecting you because, well, because you're you – they consider you the prize. I'm seen as the competition and I even got coffee spilt on me this morning because of it."

"What?!" he said incredulously, scanning my clothing.

"It's fine. You can't see it," I waved him off, "I just can't be seen with you right now."

Elliot let out a huff and shifted on his feet, "Listen. I am one hundred percent in agreement that we have behave professionally in the office. But I don't see why we can't still at least train together at lunch time. I have never seen one of those girls on the running track or in the gym, and last I checked there's no policy against exercising with a co-worker of the opposite sex.

"It was great training with you last week Katrina, and if you will at least continue to do that with me then we can get to know each other a little better and see where this all takes us."

"I don't know Elliot; I think our hormones might be clouding our judgement here a bit."

"Well, I know they're clouding mine," he said stepping closer to me and lowering his voice, "the whole time you've been talking to me, I can't stop thinking about having those long legs of yours wrapped around my waist again." His closeness was intoxicating as I breathed him in; his body scent mixed with his deodorant was earthy and raw. I closed my eyes and forced myself to push away from him, placing my hand on his chest to stop him moving closer to me.

"Fine, I'll train with you," my voice came out embarrassingly breathy, and I could see his eyes darken with arousal. "But this," I gestured between us, "this attraction between us, needs to be kept in check for now. We can't go around stealing kisses from each other when we think no one's watching. That's not why I brought you in here."

He stepped away and let out a slow breath, running his hands through his hair, scratching the back of his head.

"Ok, it's a deal," he said.

"Well then I will see you at the gym on Friday?" He nodded in reply. "Wait here and I'll go ahead. We don't need to be seen coming out of the stairwell together. They'll have a field day with that."

Chapter 10

Over the next few weeks things did calm down at work, I didn't go back to Friday night drinks and tried to spend as little time in the break room as possible, opting to leave the library five minutes early to make my coffee and bring it to my desk to drink while I surfed the net or called David or my mum for a chat. Kayley would stop in on her way back from the kitchen each day but said that she understood why I wanted to stay away for the moment. She was just disappointed as she liked having me around.

Training was going well. I was getting to know Elliot better; I learned that he was 25 and that his parents were divorced. He went into law because his father was a barrister, so he had a lot to live up to and felt fairly pressured by him to be as successful, if not more.

His mother didn't work, she lived in Parramatta with her new husband while Elliot lived in his Dad's flat in Bondi. His father had moved in with his fiancé but continued to pay Elliot's housing costs. Actually, his dad paid for everything.

I found that amazing because my brother, and I paid board to continue living in our childhood home the moment we started working – I couldn't imagine having a credit card attached to my parent's account to use freely.

I also came to learn that he used to be a really chubby kid all the way through to his mid-teens. But when he started kayaking, he dropped the extra kilograms. All of a sudden, he got attention from girls and didn't really know how to deal with it. So he learned how to become indifferent to keep them at an arm's length, only choosing to date a handful of girls.

"You don't even know how hot you are, do you?" I asked him one day while we were out running.

"I know how hot you are," he replied with a devilish grin before changing the subject, "When are you going to let me take you out?"

"Soon," was all I gave him. "Hey, did you know our mothers know each other?"

"I did."

"You did?! Hmmm, it's a small world isn't it?"

"Sure is."

"Elliot?"

"Yes?"

"You didn't tell your mother anything about what's going on with us did you?"

"What is going on with us Katrina?" he asked seriously.

"Well, just that we're hanging out – training, you know, getting to know each other," I replied, squirming a little under his gaze.

"Yes, I have told her about you."

"Oh, did she say if she spoke to my mum about it? I only ask because I haven't told my mum anything yet and well, she gets a little… too involved, in my personal life sometimes."

"No she hasn't said that she spoke to your mum, but she did tell me to be gentle with you and not to break your heart."

"Ok…Why? Do you make it a habit to go around breaking girl's hearts?"

"No, I don't actually – I thought it might have something to do with you, specifically."

And then it dawned on me, "Oh god; she *has* been talking to my mother, and my mother has been telling her my business!" I stopped running and flopped down dramatically on the grass next to the path.

Elliot stood over me, blocking the sunlight, "Is there something *you* want to tell me?"

"I really don't want to talk about it to anyone Elliot, but I think it's best if you hear this all from me instead of through the grapevine of our mothers."

He came and sat down next to me, "I'm all ears."

I took a deep breath, "What your mother was talking about – what my mother told her has to do with my scars. There's a bit more to the story than what I've already told you." I sat up and hugged my knees to my chest as Elliot sat quietly beside me listening. "I was in a pretty serious relationship not all that long ago. His name was Christopher, and he was a fair bit older than me. Things got serious pretty quickly and next thing I knew we were living together. I knew I was too young, but I figured why wait. My parents were very supportive – especially my mother; she absolutely adored him.

"He had always had a bit of a problem with my friendship with David, and I thought it was just a bit of jealousy and that eventually, for my sake, they would learn to get along. I had hoped Christopher would see that what David and I had was purely platonic.

"After we had been living together for a month David and Christopher had an argument, after which, Christopher refused to allow David back into our apartment. We fought about it and I told him that David was my best friend, and that I wouldn't be giving him up.

"Things started to go from bad to worse and Christopher would go on rages whenever he saw me talking to another guy, which was hard for me because I've always spent so much time around guys when I'm training and racing.

"On the night I left him, David was over watching a movie with me. Christopher was supposed to be at work, so we thought it would all be safe, and I could spend some quality time with my friend. Well, as you can probably guess, Christopher came home from work early and lost his mind. He was a really big strong guy, and he walked straight over, punched David in the face, picked him up like a rag doll and threw him out of the door and into the hallway.

"He then turned his wrath on me, he told me that I was nothing but a common gutter slut, and that I couldn't be trusted. He grabbed me by the back of my hair and ran with me, slamming me through the glass sliding door, which is how I got all of my scars.

"Next, he started punching me and was supposedly trying rape me – I don't remember much past going through the glass - but David managed to save me. He kicked a hole through the door to unlock it and get back in, grabbed a frying pan from the kitchen and whacked Christopher over the head with it, knocking him out cold.

"Like I said, I don't really remember much after going through the glass, just what David saw and the doctors told me happened based on my injuries. I lost a lot of blood because the glass slit one of my wrists, but David got me to the emergency room faster than any ambulance could have come to get me, so I was ok in the end.

"I know I told you when you asked about my scars that stupidity was the reason I went through the glass, and really it was. It was stupid of me to move in with him and even more stupid for me to stay when he started to get volatile. I should have gone back home instead of fighting back. None of it would have happened if I wasn't being so forthright and stubborn."

Elliot sat next to me in deathly silence. I hadn't looked at him the whole time I was relaying my story, and only now chanced a look at his face. His brows were tightly knit, and his face was a swirl of emotions. I wasn't sure if he was going to cry in sorrow or explode with anger.

"So let me get this straight," Elliot spoke through clenched teeth. "Some guy puts you into hospital, and you think it's your fault for provoking him?"

I shook my head, "No Elliot. I know it wasn't my fault. I just think that if I wasn't so caught up in fighting with him over my friendship with David - or any other guy, for that matter; that it all could have been avoided...I think I should have paid attention to the situation and left... I think I never should have moved in with him in the first place."

"Did you at least press charges against the guy?" he asked expectantly.

"No, I didn't," I said looking the other way, everyone in my life was disappointed with me for not pressing charges. "I don't even know why I didn't. I guess I just wanted it all to be over.

"No else knows this, but he came to visit me at the hospital.

He was so upset about what he had done that my heart kind of broke for him. He told me he had started taking steroids because he saw me joking with one of the body builders from the gym and thought I was flirting. It was all ridiculous in the end. I told him that I wouldn't press charges, as long as he was out of the apartment when I went to collect my things, which he was, so..." I shrugged my shoulders, not really having anything else to say.

Elliot turned to face me and took my arm in his hands, turning it over to inspect my scars, touching each one tentatively with his fingertips. My heart skittered across my chest as he lifted my hand and pressed a soft kiss to the scar at my wrist. Sliding his hand up my arm, he traced the scar on my shoulder before kissing me there too, sending waves of longing throughout my body.

I became unable to resist him any longer when, using his thumb, he caressed the scar on my face. Closing my eyes as an intoxicating wave of desire flooded through me, I leaned into his hand, not caring where we were and ignoring the fact that we shouldn't be touching like this out in the open.

I let him kiss me, at first I didn't fully respond, but as he gently sucked my lip with his, I parted my lips and let out a soft gasp, allowing him in. My body was on fire as his arms circled around me, as I moved to sit on his lap, never breaking the kiss.

Our tongues danced together as they explored the crevices of each other's mouths, replacing the pain I felt from telling that story with something so much sweeter and more beautiful than anything I had ever experienced.

My head tipped back as he rained kisses down my neck and across my chest, leaving a tiny trail of fire in their wake. Our breathing was getting heavy, and I could feel his arousal pressing against my own, causing me to grind instinctively against him. He moaned and captured my mouth in his again, hugging me tighter to him as his hands caressed the exposed skin on my back.

A sudden beeping brought us crashing back to reality along with the comprehension of where we were and what we were doing. Panting, I sat back as he slowly released me so I could switch off my alarm.

"I guess I had better get back," I breathed, laughing a little.

His eyes were dark as he reached his hands up to my face and pulled me towards him kissing me deeply again. He gently brushed the hair away from my face as he searched my eyes for the answers to questions unasked. His eyes narrowed a touch before he said, "Now we can go."

"You are going to be our undoing Elliot Roberts."

His eyes sparkled as he laughed, "As far as I can tell I'm already undone by you."

Standing, he held out his hand to help me up. I did a quick scan of the park, hoping no one had seen us here and chanced one last brief kiss. "I'll go ahead like I normally do ok?"

He nodded, "I might sit back down here and while and ah… calm down a bit." I looked down and noticed his erection tenting his running shorts; I raised my eyebrows and couldn't stop the grin from curling the sides of my mouth.

"I think that might be a good idea," I said laughing as I started moving off.

"Katrina," I stopped and turned to face him, "you know I'd never hurt you right?"

"I do know Elliot. I wouldn't be spending time with you if I thought you would. Don't go feeling sorry for me Elliot, I'm fine." I called out as I ran ahead of him.

***

"So, how is tennis?" I asked my mother when we got a quiet moment alone, it was after dinner on Wednesday night, and I was helping her with the dishes while my brother and father had taken a trip up to our local shops to get some ice cream for dessert.

She kept her focus on the dish she was scrubbing as she spoke, "It's fine, my game's getting better, I think."

"Have you been making friends with the other women?" I probed.

"Well yes, I've met them all for coffee a couple of times, and I went to that dinner a few weeks ago. They're a really nice group." She glanced at me and gave me a quick smile.

I narrowed my eyes as she turned away, the gentle approach wasn't working. I would have to be more direct if I was going to find out what she had been saying to Elliot's mother.

"What about that lady you were telling me about? The one with a son at my work - how do you get along with her?"

"Oh you mean Kathy? She's great. We get along really well."

"Do you talk about your children?"

She shifted nervously and continued to talk into the sink, "Of course we do Katrina. It's what mothers talk about most."

"Any interesting topics?" I ventured.

She stopped and turned to face me, "I'm guessing you're aware that I know how you spend your lunch times at work – is that what this is about?"

"Partly."

"I have to be honest Katrina. I am a bit hurt that you haven't told me anything about Elliot yet. How long has it been? A month? More?"

"We're not together yet mum."

"That's not how his mother tells it; she says you're seeing each other."

"I'm not really sure what we are to each other right now, I'm just spending time with him."

"Katrina, I'm really happy that you are spending time with a boy, or a man in his case, but I am upset with you. Elliot is what? 25? And he has told his mother about you. You are my *daughter*, and you haven't told me anything. You acted like you didn't even know him."

I had to admit it sounded pretty bad when she put it like that, "I'm sorry mum. I just didn't want to talk about it until I knew it was something."

Her mouth twitched at the corners, threatening a smile, but she kept it under control and asked hopefully, "Are you saying it's something now?"

"I'm saying it's something now." Her face changed from stern to excited in milliseconds. She let out a little girl squeal and hugged me tightly.

"I'm so glad you are moving on! Tell me about him, when do I get to meet him?"

"Mum, slow down ok. We're not up to that stage yet. He is really nice though, you would like him. Although I have to ask mum, have you told Kathy about what happened to me with Christopher?" Her eyes dropped immediately, I could tell by the look on her face that she had.

"I'm sorry, I told her before I knew that you were seeing each other. She didn't tell him did she?"

"No, she just warned him to be gentle with me, so I thought it best that I told him myself."

"How did he take it?"

I shrugged, "He was angry, and kind of sad about it. I think he was worried that I might have thought he could be capable of doing the same thing."

"And do you think he is?"

I shook my head vigorously before I answered, "He doesn't seem to have the bad-boy streak in him that Christopher did, so no. I don't think he would."

"Well, if his mother is anything to go by I don't think he'd be like Christopher either."

"I just don't like people feeling sorry for me, you know. He sees me as really strong and capable because that's what I always show him, and now he knows some guy beat me up. I don't want him to think I am weak and need protecting all of a sudden."

"I doubt he sees it that way, sweetheart."

"I hope not."

Chapter 11

Friday had come around again and I was planning to stop by the conference room for a drink that evening, after not attending for a little over a month.

I had instead, been going out with David every Friday night to have dinner and go dancing before catching the two o'clock train home, drunk and exhausted on Saturday morning. It was wreaking havoc on my training schedule, but I didn't have any big races planned until January, meaning that I was happy to have a bit of fun for now.

Most mornings I would catch the train to work with David so I advised him of my plans that morning, and never being one to miss out of a good time, he wanted to come along as well.

Elliot was next on my list to inform, I told him when we were training up in the gym at lunch time, while we were doing sit ups and throwing a medicine ball at each other.

"Is that wise?" he asked cautiously, as he threw the ball to me.

I caught it and leaned back with it over my head, hefting it up to return it before I answered. He caught it quickly, stopping the exercise to listen. "Yeah, I think I need to show them I can go, and that you and I can be normal around each other. You've been going every week haven't you?"

"Yeah I have, I normally stop in for a drink, so I can talk to the partners – networking; you know?"

I nodded my understanding and went on, "Well, I thought that if I go, stay close to Kayley and head out with them afterwards - without you; that it may just end any 'supposing' about things going on between us."

"Without me huh?" he noted with his eyebrows raised.

I tilted my head slightly, frowning as I reasoned, "You know we can't go out with them all together. Bianca and Beth will most likely be there, and then we'll get hauled into Priya's office again – I doubt she'll let us off this time."

"It's ok – don't worry about it. I was planning on meeting up with some old uni friends afterwards anyway. Although, if you get bored hanging around that lot, I'll be at the Docks Hotel." He raised the ball above his head to resume the exercise, lying back before throwing the ball again for me to catch.

It was my turn to pause after catching the ball, still having more to say. "Tempting, but I won't be able to - I have to catch the train back with David at two. But, I was going to ask you if you were free Saturday night."

His eyes widened in happy surprise, "You're going to let me take you out?" he asked.

I smiled 'yes' at him, relishing in the delight I felt at his thrilled response.

He leaned closer to me and lowered his voice, "Although, what do you think about staying in and having dinner at my place?" he suggested.

Those pictures of what I'd do to him when we were alone started flitting through my mind, and it was my turn to feel excited, "I think, considering our track record with PDA so far, dinner at your place would be a very good idea."

***

David was waiting for me at reception this time, so he didn't have to James Bond his way through to the conference room.

His eyebrows shot up as he let out a low whistle when he saw me. "I hope you weren't wearing that all day," he commented taking me by the hand and twirling me around. "You look gorgeous, Trina."

I had gone shopping earlier that week and bought a skirt that transformed into a short black strapless dress. I wore it with a thick belt in the centre to cinch in my waist and give me the appearance of curves. I let Kayley help me with my makeup and hair, then put on some strappy high heels so I was then standing eye level with David.

Taking him by the hand, I led him into the conference room where everyone was already drinking and chatting amicably. What they spoke of, I have no clue. I struggled to maintain focus the moment I caught Elliot watching me from across the room.

The conversation around me was becoming more of a humming despite the energy I was exerting in an attempt to listen to it. I could feel his eyes boring into me, the awareness filling my body and numbing the sounds to silence around me, so I was attuned only to him.

"Katrina!"

I blinked surprised, "What!? Huh?" I blundered out, as my attention was dragged back by David, standing in front of me, attempting to hand me a drink.

"Where the hell were you just now? I was trying to hand that thing to you for a while." He told me as I relieved him of the glass he was holding out.

I took a mouthful of the cold liquid and laughed uneasily, "I don't know, I just kind of switched off for a while – long week; you know?"

The great thing about Friday drinks was that people relaxed and showed a side of themselves they didn't normally show around the office, even the partners were laughing and smiling - acting more or less human. As the night moved on, we all gathered around the conference table and talked as though we were long-time friends.

One of the partners Ken, a small man with mousy brown, curly hair - that bounced as he moved his head; came and sat in the chair next to me to spark up a conversation. He was wearing a tie covered in Looney Tunes characters, finding it a refreshing change to the usual spots and stripes; I complimented him on his choice.

Thanking me, he asked if I was at university, to which I replied yes, I was studying law. Politely, he asked me about my grades and which area of law I was most interested in. I told him that at that moment I liked family law. He himself practiced patent and trademark law and said that he would find family law difficult to handle as there were too many emotions involved.

"Although, I don't think it would be as hard as criminal law like Elliot here is learning to practise," Ken boomed bringing Elliot into our conversation. He had been unobtrusively sitting across from us, nursing his drink and acting as though he was watching the room.

"I don't know about that Ken. They can both have their ups and downs I think."

"That is probably very true. I am lucky; I spend my days looking at names, slogans and devices. None of that gets too personal so it's easy to do well and leave your work at the office." He sat back in his chair and looked at his watch, "Ah, it's getting late – almost ten already. I think we had better call it a night or my wife will lock me out of the house," he joked, slapping his thighs as he hefted himself out of the chair, leaving Elliot and I, sitting across from each other.

As I looked at him, my breathing quickened. The attraction between us so strong that I struggled with acting upon the hot image of me leaping across the table and ripping his shirt open to run my tongue down his…*stop it!*

I briefly closed my eyes to straighten my thoughts, opening them to give Elliot a quick smile before rising to put some distance between us, preventing me from doing something foolish in front of so many prying eyes.

Ken stood at the front of the room, loudly telling everyone that it was time to head off. I took the opportunity to wander over to David, who was standing by the bar talking to Bianca, Beth and Carl.

"Hey Trina," David said happily to me, he was already a little soused, taking advantage of the free liquor before we headed out. Bianca and Beth said nothing to me, instead choosing to excuse themselves so they could visit the ladies' room before we all left.

Carl nudged me with his shoulder and said out of the side of his mouth "Well, you just chased them away."

I gave him a little shrug and walked with him and David to the reception area where everyone was gathering to go to Pontoon together. Elliot walked past with Andrew and Carmen. They were all saying their goodbyes to the rest of us.

"Aren't you coming with us this time?" asked David.

"No, not this time," Elliot answered as his eyes flicked to me and then back to David, "I'm going out to a late dinner with these two, then I have some friends to meet up with. Have a good night though." He nodded politely, and walked to the elevator bay where Carmen and Andrew were already waiting.

David put his arm around me and gave my shoulders a squeeze, "You ready to dance the night away baby girl? Although I don't know how I'm going to keep the guys away from you in that dress," he said biting on his lower lip and shaking his head, making appreciative noises.

"Do you think it shows too much leg?" I asked seriously.

"There's always too much leg with you Trina, those things go on forever."

"You make me sound like a spider!" I grumbled pushing him on the shoulder.

He laughed at me pulling me closer as Bianca and Beth re-joined us.

"Is everyone ready?" Kayley called out.

There was a chorous of 'yes' and 'let's go' as we all moved as a group to catch the next lift down and walk to the bar.

As it was last time, the bar was packed and people were spilling out onto the surrounding patio area. Kayley started waving her arm above her head animatedly as she saw her friends and cousin, Connor. *Oh shit, I didn't even consider him being here,* I thought.

They were sitting at one of the outdoor bench tables and moved around so we could join them. Baskets of hot chips sat on the table that weren't quite finished and were offered to us, having not eaten dinner yet we all dug in voraciously.

I could see Connor watching me and wondered if I should apologise for running off on him last time. Although, movement against my side drew my attention as I felt David's body jostling as he laughed. I turned to see what was so funny, feeling slightly deflated when I realised he was chatting into Beth's ear, sharing some sort of joke that no one else was in on.

I looked over at Bianca, who looked woefully unhappy – if she wasn't such a bitch to me, I might have felt sorry for her. When she stood up to ask if anyone wanted to dance, I stood up along with the majority of the table. I didn't want to watch David's seduction of Beth either.

Separating from the group, I went to get a drink from the bar. As I lined up, I was forced to push my way forward or risk missing out entirely. It was such an effort that I decided to buy four black Russians at once. Standing to the side, I held two drinks stacked in each hand, transferring my straw between each glass as I drained the one before.

"Thirsty?" an Irish accent asked me. I looked up to see Connor standing in front of me smiling.

Releasing the straw, I let out a nervous laugh, "Well, I want a buzz while I dance, and I don't want to keep lining up."

"I have to say I like the system you have going on there."

"Thank you, laziness is the mother of invention and all that – no; that's not how it goes," I frowned, the alcohol already coursing through my veins and joining with the couple of drinks I'd had at work.

"I think you mean 'necessity' – necessity is the mother of all invention," he laughed.

I sucked on the last of my drink and winked at him, "That's the one." On my seventh drink for the night, my body was well and truly buzzing with the effects.

"Are you planning on dancing tonight? I'll try not to chase you off this time," he intimated.

"Oh that wasn't you Connor, that was one hundred per cent me," I assured him. If it wasn't for Elliot, I think I would gladly have let this Irish man win me over. He had this mischievous glint to his eyes that promised a good time. I wanted to go and have a good time with him, but I wanted Elliot more.

"You go and dance, I'll finish up here and have a bit of a look around. But, I'll see you out there later," I suggested.

His jovial face dulled a little as disappointment showed behind his smile. I felt a momentary pang of guilt from leading him on last time as I watched him return to the dance floor.

Placing my now empty glasses on the nearest table, I started to push my way outside to find David, spotting him before I made it out the door. He was on the dance floor with Beth leaning up against him. He was behind her with his hand around her waist moving to the music with his head dipped towards her neck. She seemed to be loving it. I didn't love it; it bothered me; it bothered me a lot – why did he need to pick up the girls from my work? Out of all the girls here, why did he have to pick her?

Bianca saw me watching and smirked, she then blatantly

moved over to Connor and started to dance with him, moving him away from the group and shooting glances my way whenever she could. I supposed she was showing me she could steal men from me, although, I could never actually claim to know what went on inside that girls head.

I stood watching her dance with Connor and Beth with David. My irritation swirling inside my stomach and rising throughout my body until something inside me clicked, I needed to take action.

Lacking the mental faculties, due to my slight intoxication, to stop myself, I marched right up onto the dance floor and started dancing in Connor's line of sight. Something told me that getting him away from Bianca would piss all three of them off. It was selfish of me, I know, but at the time I wasn't focusing on the fact that I was using Connor... again. I just wanted to strike out some way, and I didn't really care how.

When he caught my eye, I smiled seductively at him, closing my eyes to let the music flow through me as I danced. That's all it took to switch his attention to me.

He sidled up behind me, slipping his hands around my waist and moving side to side with me. I lifted my arms and let them drop, running my hands lightly over his head before I opened my eyes slightly to see that Bianca's dance had dropped to a slow bounce, as she remerged with the group.

Sway by sway, Connor led me deeper into the throng. We danced together until my saliva grew thick, and the ache in my feet could no longer be ignored.

"I need water!" I yelled over the music. Connor nodded, and taking my hand, he led me through the crowd, toward the bar. He went to pay, but I shook my head no and paid for both instead.

Looking a little surprised, he nodded his thanks, inclining his head to ask if I wanted to go outside to the table we had been sitting at earlier. I nodded yes, and he followed me out with his hand resting at the small of my back.

As soon as we were outside the noise wasn't quite so booming, but we still had to lean close to be heard, our ears still humming from the deafening sound inside. He leaned into me and said, "I really want to kiss you, but I'm afraid you'll run off again."

I laughed and replied, "I think you should listen to your fears on that one."

He sat back and looked at me thoughtfully. "You know. I don't normally have that reaction on beautiful women such as yourself."

I tilted my head and smiled, picking up a bottle cap from the table, twisting it with my fingers. "That's because they probably all swoon over your accent. They'd be putty in your hands."

He sat forward again, closing the small distance between us so he could speak softer in my ear. "Well why isn't it working on you? Is it because of that guy from last time? Or is it because of that guy dancing with Beth?"

I laughed nervously, "Maybe," I answered, scrunching my nose up a bit. "I don't really want to talk about it though if that's ok."

"That's fine, but you're breaking my heart here."

"I'm sorry I'm not meaning to. I do like you – it's just all a bit… complicated."

He moved my hair behind my shoulder and said, "I can wait until it's uncomplicated."

I laughed through my nose replying, "That could take a while."

He shrugged and smiled like it was no big deal, "There're

plenty of girls to keep me busy in the meantime," he told me with a lopsided grin.

I laughed as I took a swig of my water, "Be careful Connor, your dick will fall off."

He returned my laughter, "You ready to go back in?"

I looked at my watch; it was one-thirty in the morning, "No. I'd better find David, so we can catch the train home."

I went back inside to where I had last seen him on the dance floor and couldn't find him, I scanned the bar and didn't see him there either. Pulling my phone out of my bag, I tapped out a message. **Where are you???**

Pushing through the crowds with Connor following close by, I searched in every corner for him, coming back empty. I checked my phone again and found no reply. *Shit!*

"I need to go outside and make a phone call," I yelled to Connor.

"I'll come with you."

"Don't, I'll be fine."

He indicated that he didn't care, and that he was coming

anyway so I dragged him back out with me again, further onto the wharf to try to hear over the music.

I tried to call David and got no answer. Instead, I got his voicemail – after listening to his upbeat message, I left an irate voicemail to tell him that he was going to make us miss the train. I then tried calling Carmen to see if she was still in town, so I could at least ride the train back with her, but I just got her voicemail as well.

"FUCK!" I stomped my foot like a petulant child.

"Listen, I've heard stories about what happens on the train line, and I don't think it's safe for you to catch it home on your own. How about, we wait and see if David shows up before the next train, and if he doesn't you can just come home and stay with me for tonight?" The look on his face was sincere enough, but I was pretty sure I knew why he wanted me there.

I laughed at his boldness, "That's really nice of you Connor, but I have met you twice and my parents would pitch a fit."

"That's fair enough," he conceded. "How about we go back inside and ask around for your friend David, surely someone would have seen him leave – he's a pretty tall guy."

I agreed, and we pushed our way through the crowds again,

asking everyone we knew if they had seen David leaving. An hour later and still no luck, I hadn't gotten a text from him and when I called once more, it didn't even ring, it went straight to voicemail.

Weighing my options, I could wait around until closing time in the hope that David would show up, or I could catch the train home on my own, but the western suburbs line wasn't the safest train line at three o'clock on a Saturday morning, not to mention waiting around the front of the station to catch a cab home on my own. It would be better if I could stay with someone else for the night. I realised there was only one person my mother would be ok with me going to because she was friends with his mother.

Chapter 12

Taking a deep breath, I scrolled through my contacts list and put a call through to Elliot, hoping he wasn't somewhere too loud to hear the ring.

"Hey, I was hoping you'd call – what time is it?" he asked groggily. I could hear the smile in his voice, and he sounded sleepy.

"Did I wake you?"

"It's fine, don't worry about it. What's up?"

"I'm kind of stranded. I can't find David, and I don't really want to catch the train all the way home on my own."

Without missing a beat he said, "I'll come and get you."

"Are you sure?"

"I'm sure, can you get to the casino?"

"Hang on," I put my hand over the phone and asked Connor, "How far is it to walk to Star City?"

"15 - 20 minutes?" he said.

"Yeah I can make it there."

"Who are you with?"

"Kayley's cousin."

"It isn't that guy you were dancing with last time is it?" my silence answered for me. "Are you serious!" he exclaimed, sounding annoyed.

"Are you coming to get me or not?" I asked, not reacting to his change in tone.

He sighed, "Yes. I'm coming. Meet me outside the sports bar."

"Alright, I'm on my way." I pressed the end call button and looked at Connor.

"So he's the complication hey?"

"Something like that," I smiled reticently, "I have to get to the casino, which way do I go?"

"You are seriously planning on walking there by yourself?"

"It's only 15 minutes. I'll be fine. It's safer than catching the train on my own."

"Don't be ridiculous, I'll walk you."

"Connor, no, I can't ask you to do that."

"You aren't asking Katrina. I'm insisting. Now let me just tell the others to wait until I get back." He trotted over to the table where some of his friends were still sitting, leaning down to talk to them, inclining his head towards me as he spoke. One guy gave him a pat on the back, and he returned to me to the tune of cat calls from the table.

"What did you just tell them?" I asked him, an accusatory tone to my voice.

"Nothing really, I just said that I was taking you somewhere for a ride."

My mouth dropped open, and he started laughing at me.

"I'm joking, I'm joking! I would never lie about sex with you Katrina. I will wait my turn like a man." I gave him a very unimpressed look, "Seriously though, I just told them I was going to walk you to your car. That's all"

"That's all?"

He nodded earnestly. "Shall we?" he asked, gesturing for me to walk with him.

"Thanks, Connor. For walking me," I told him after a while.

"It's no trouble, can't have your mugging on my conscience…So, um, this guy we're meeting, why wasn't he with you tonight?"

"That's the complicated part."

"I see. You work together and there's that no dating thing at your office right?"

I gave him a confused look.

"Kayley told me about it, that's how I know."

"Oh ok, I can't really talk about it though Connor. We could both lose our jobs if people think we're dating."

"I'm not going to tell anyone Katrina, I don't want to be the reason you lose your job. Besides that would be counterproductive on my part wouldn't it?"

"Oh yeah, how so?"

"Well, if you get fired, you won't be coming out with Kayley anymore so I won't get to see you and continue working my Irish charm on you. Plus, statistically office romances don't tend to work out so I want to make sure I'm around to swoop in and pick up the pieces when the inevitable happens," he grinned.

I laughed at him, "Well, as long as your motives are pure."

"They are pure – purely in my own self-interest!"

We arrived at the front entrance to Star City Casino, and I turned to him again to say thank you.

"You're sure you don't want me to walk you in?" he asked.

"I'll be fine. Thank you for walking me Connor." I leaned toward him and gave him a chaste kiss on the cheek.

"It was my pleasure Katrina. I hope to see you again soon," he said, as he stood and watched until I had walked through the doors, before he left to return to his friends.

Elliot was already there when I reached the sports bar, leaning up against the wall outside it looking at his phone. He was wearing a pair of faded blue jeans and a white v-neck t-shirt. His hair was sticking up and messy from sleeping - he looked positively delicious.

The corridor we were in was pretty quiet so the clack of my heels could be heard as I walked towards him, alerting him to my presence. He stood up properly and gave me the most brilliant smile I have ever seen on him. It made my chest swell, and I impulsively started to run to him, jumping into his arms as he captured me in a passionate kiss that had me melting on the spot.

He broke away and smiled at me, brushing my hair out of my face. "I was dreaming about you when you called me," he murmered.

A little ripple skittered through my stomach and shot down between my legs. "Good dreams I hope," I purred, leaning into him.

"Let's get out of here, and I'll show you"

The sexual tension was ubiquitous on the drive home, it was hard for me to keep myself in my seat and not jump in his lap to ride him while he drove. He told me to wait when he pulled over and got out of the car, walking around to my side to help me out. Holding my hand, he led me to the entrance of a block of brown brick flats, it was dark and fairly surrounded by trees, so I couldn't see much, but I could hear the whoosh of the ocean as I waited for him to unlock the main door.

"How far away from the ocean are you?" I couldn't help but ask.

"One street," he replied, "you can see the beach from the balcony." We climbed the beige carpeted stairs quietly and stopped in front of a brown wooden door at the top of the second flight.

"This is it," he said looking back over his shoulder at me. With a click the door was open, and we stepped inside a narrow hall. The door swung shut, and he turned and pinned me to it, his arms either side of me. I couldn't stop the smile from spreading over my face as he looked hungrily into my eyes, clamping his mouth down on mine as he kissed me deeply. I slid my arms around his neck and pressed myself to him curling my fingers through the back of his already messy hair.

He reached his hands down to my backside and hoisted me up, so I had to wrap my legs around his waist. He carried me down the hallway, past a formal dining room, kissing me all the way until he reached the lounge room and set me down, kneeling in front of me. Only then did he pause and look at me.

"You drive me wild, Katrina."

He smoothed my hair away from my face and started to kiss a trail down my neck and chest, his hands moving to cup my small breasts and squeeze my already hard nipples. I let out a short moan as I leaned my body into his hands, wanting more from him. He pulled my dress aside and took one little bud into his mouth causing me to drop my head back and moan with pleasure. Guiding me until I was lying, he slid his hand down my body and between my thighs, I parted them willingly as I felt his fingertips brush the edges of my thoroughly damp panties.

He slipped his fingers under the elastic waistband, over my mound and between my folds, to the slick wetness of my arousal. I gasped as I felt his fingers enter me, rocking my hips to the motion of his hand as it moved in and out of me. He continued to circle his tongue around my nipple as he circled his finger around my already swollen clit. I thought I was going to explode then and there and started to moan my pending orgasm.

"Not yet," he whispered to me re-covering my breasts before getting up off the couch to scoop me up again and carry me to the bedroom.

I watched his handsome face as he carried me to the bed; I had never before been made to feel this light and girly before.

It was incredible for a girl my size to be carried like I weighed nothing, and a complete turn on.

"You're amazing," I breathed as he set me down, like precious cargo, on the bed.

"Reserve your judgement for when we're finished. I haven't done this for a while."

He didn't give me time to wonder how long it had been before he leaned down to kiss me deeply yet again, his tongue probing my mouth and dancing with mine. I caught his bottom lip in my teeth and gently sucked as he pulled away.

"Do you know how hard it was not to react to you in that dress tonight?" he said to me as he undid my belt and tossed it aside. "I wanted so much just to slide my hands up those impossibly long legs of yours and have my way with you in front of everyone." He gripped the top of my dress and slid it down to expose my breasts fully. I lifted my hips a little to aid him, as he slipped my dress down the length of my body and dropped it on the floor.

He stood and removed his own shirt and jeans, revealing the well-toned body that I knew was under there. Every bit of him was hard, and I mean every bit. My mouth watered just looking at him. I moved to sit, desperately wanting to run my hands down his chest and over his rippling stomach and down to his…

"Lay back down," he instructed. Obligingly, I did as he said. He slid his hands along my legs to hook his fingers into my panties and slide them off in one dramatic pull. He flicked them over his shoulder and grinned devilishly at me.

Kneeling on the floor, he grabbed my legs, dragging them either side of him so his face could fit comfortably between them. I let out my breath, slowly anticipating his mouth on me.

"Tell me you want me Katrina," he breathed.

I didn't even hesitate, "I want you Elliot. I want you desperately," I gasped out.

He let out a moan of his own as he buried his face between my legs, hungrily lapping at my juices and lightly flicking his tongue over my clit causing me to twitch my hips in response.

"Oh god, I can't take much more of this!" I called grabbing his head and holding him to me. He sucked at my clit and swirled his tongue, teasing my entrance with his fingers.

I called out his name, gripping his head tightly between my thighs as I exploded, bucking against him as he drove his fingers inside me, curling them forward to rub that sensitive spot inside. I could feel another orgasm mounting and called to the heavens this time as I exploded once more. He wiped at his mouth and then climbed back on top of me, kissing me deeply so I could taste myself in his mouth.

He reached over to a bedside drawer and pulled out a condom sitting back as he applied it over his long thick shaft while I watched unabashedly. He crept over me and held his weight, his arms either side of me as he nudged his tip at my entrance, locking my eyes with his, studying me. I lifted my hips to nudge him closer, and he drove himself inside me with one movement. We gasped together at the erotic intensity of being connected so deeply as he moved himself in and out of me in time with my own hips rocking.

Each time he drove into me, I moaned from the pleasure of it, "Do you think I can get you to come again?" he panted in my ear.

"Keep going like this and you will," I gasped out in return.

His steady rhythm was pushing and pulling at my insides, building my pleasure to the verge of exploding once more. I clenched reflexively.

"Oh god, I don't think I can hold on if you keep doing that."

"Oh! Just hold on, hold on!" I cried out as I clenched tighter and my orgasm burst through me for a third time.

He breathed out slowly as he shuddered, I could feel him pulsing inside of me as we collapsed together, gasping for breath, our limbs all tangled up with each other.

"See - I was right," I remarked, trailing my fingers up his back. "You are amazing."

He lifted his head and smiled brightly at me, "No, you are." He kissed me again slowly this time, beginning to move inside me once more. I could feel his erection harden inside of me, and I gasped as he slowly ground his hips into mine.

I wrapped my legs around his middle and pulled him tightly inside me. He lifted me off the bed so that I was sitting on him, rocking with him as I looked into his eyes and could see his passion for me, his wanting of me. This time I didn't climax, but it was beautiful, sweet and slow.

He got up and removed his condom, wrapping it in a tissue and dropping it in the bin in the adjoining bathroom. I couldn't keep my eyes off his body and watched him shamelessly as he moved back towards the bed. Putting his arm around my waist, he dragged me towards him, wrapping himself around me, nuzzling my neck.

"Sleep, beautiful," he muttered against my skin. I wriggled to get comfortable, feeling safe in this cocoon that his body had created around me as I drifted off into a peaceful sleep.

Chapter 13

I was pulled from my sleep by the sound of my phone ringing, the caller ID revealing it to be my mother. "Shit," I said to myself, realising I forgot to call her last night to tell her I wasn't going home.

I cleared the sleepiness from my throat and answered quietly, trying not to disturb Elliot, still sleeping, beside me. "Are you out training already?" my mother asked immediately.

I felt relieved that she hadn't realised I didn't come home and was about to go along, when I realised I'd have to go home in my dress and heels later. Elliot stirred, opening one eye, sleepily watching me. I smoothed my hand all the way down his still naked body as I got up from the bed.

"Uh hi mum, no I'm not training." I picked up the dress I had been wearing last night and quickly tugged it on, signalling to Elliot that I was going to go into the lounge room to talk to my mother.

"Well where are you? It's six o'clock in the morning, and your car's not here." She gasped as she realised what was going on, "You didn't even come home last night did you?"

"No, mum, I'm um… with Elliot," I admitted as I sat down on the brown leather L shaped couch and tucked my feet under my body.

Suddenly, her whole demeanour changed, and I could hear the smile in her voice, "Oh my goodness! Was it wonderful? Kathy showed me his photo yesterday, and he is so attractive," she gushed.

"Mum!"

"What?"

"I'm not going to tell you that stuff," I spoke quietly into the phone, not wanting Elliot to overhear.

"Sorry, it's just a bit exciting isn't it?"

"I suppose so."

"I'll talk to you when you get home then, you are coming home aren't you?"

"I'm not sure yet. I'll call you later to let you know though."

"Alright, just make sure you tell me this time ok? I got a bit of a shock this morning when I woke up, and you weren't here."

"I'm sorry for worrying you mum."

"That's ok sweetheart, have a good time."

We disconnected, and I smiled at my phone thinking about my mum and her love of romance.

I got up and walked into the small kitchen to grab a glass of water. Feeling surprised at how tidy it was considering Elliot lived on his own. There wasn't even a cup in the sink.

Elliot's hands snaked around my waist as I stood facing the sink drinking my water; he kissed my neck and asked, "Everything ok?"

Setting down my glass, I turned towards him, kissing him back softly. He'd put a pair of cotton pyjama pants on and left his glorious chest bare. I ran my hand over the firmness of his pecs, "Mmmm, yeah, everything's fine. I just forgot to tell my parents that I wouldn't be home last night, so my mum was worried."

"What about your dad?"

"He's probably still asleep at this time." Elliot reached up to my face and smoothed my hair back behind my ears, gently caressing my skin with his thumbs. I closed my eyes, loving the feel of him, loving that I was finally alone with him, not having to worry if anyone could see us.

He reached down and opened the cupboard under the sink and took a new chux dishcloth out of the packet. I watched him curiously as he wet it and rubbed some hand soap into it from the dispenser he had on the window.

He then came back over to me and ever so gently started to wipe it over my face, my eyes went wide as I realised what I must look like having slept in my makeup from last night. "Oh god, I must look a fright!" I exclaimed, trying to take the cloth from him.

He moved it out of my reach, "No you look beautiful," he said kissing me quickly on the mouth, "You just don't need to wear this stuff." Ever so gently, he continued to clean off my makeup. Obligingly, I closed my eyes as he ran the cloth over my skin.

"Keep them closed," his voice was just above a whisper. I could hear him rinse the cloth to wash the soap out of it before he used it to wipe over my eyes again. "Open," I lifted my lids, blinking rapidly until they felt normal. I watched his face as he studied mine, and gently wiped the mascara from under my eyes. There was something incredibly sensual about what he was doing to me. I was finding it hard to breathe from the surge of emotion I was feeling.

I knew at this moment that the slow part of our relationship was over; I was willing to let go of the fear from my past and move forward with this man who was so strong, yet so gentle at the same time.

"There," he said when he was done. "Perfect." He brushed his knuckles along my cheek, and I caught his hand with mine, pressing a kiss to his palm.

He pulled me to him and kissed me, our tongues moving together as we moaned into each other's mouth pressing our bodies into each other.

His hands roamed down my back, and towards my buttocks where he grabbed me and hoisted me up onto the kitchen bench. Smiling into our kiss, he slid my dress up above my still naked hips. I parted my legs further as he released his erection, circling himself at my entrance and moaning because I was already tremendously wet.

When he started to push inside me, I thought fleetingly of a condom, although in that moment, I didn't care, I wanted to feel him inside me, just him and nothing else between us.

I gasped as his silken shaft slid deep inside of me, thrusting back and forth, igniting my body with a fire that felt ready to consume my senses. All there was, was him and me and I didn't think I could ever be around him without touching him again.

I wrapped my legs around him tightly, pulling him into me as he climaxed first, pulsing his juices deep inside of me. He continued to move until he was sure that I had climaxed too. It was obvious when I did because my legs gripped his waist like a vice, and I lifted myself off the bench top calling out his name.

He set me back down and left us connected, looking at me suddenly stricken, "I...I'm sorry. That's the first time I have ever done that... I don't know what came over me. I should have checked it was ok first," he babbled.

I was surprised by his reaction, "You've never had sex without a condom?"

"Never," he answered seriously.

"Well I guess that means you've got the all clear then? Health wise, I mean," I asked carefully, not really wanting to ask the difficult question but knowing how important it was for both of us to be STD free.

"Yes, I'm clear – what about you?"

"I, uh, got tested in the hospital – just to be sure, so yeah, I'm all clear. And um…I get Depo injections every six months; so I can't get pregnant," I assured him feeling awkward but glad the air was clear.

"Oh good," he breathed out his relief, kissing me again. "I don't know what it is about you; I just keep doing things that aren't normal for me." He withdrew from me, and I felt the warm gush of his semen run out of me. He looked at it and then looked at me like he didn't know what to do, *this really was the first time he had had sex without a condom.*

I told him to rinse the cloth again to clean us up. Waiting, while he insisted on doing it for both of us. When he finished, he lifted me back up from the bench top and set me on the floor before he dropped the chux into the garbage bin.

"Breakfast?" he asked me.

I nodded my agreement, and he pulled out a chair for me to sit on at the small wooden table that sat in the corner of the kitchen and only seated two. I moved over to it and sat down watching him move around the kitchen preparing toast and eggs with orange juice and coffee.

When my phone beeped that it had a message, I jumped up and retrieved it from the coffee table, where I had left it after speaking to my mother.

Not surprisingly the message was from David – **Went by ur house but ur mum said u were out. So sorry about last night, I am an idiot.**

I couldn't be angry at David because if he hadn't disappeared, then I wouldn't have just had the most intense sexual experience of my life so far.

I typed back - **Don't worry about it, just glad ur safe. Was worried.**

He messaged straight back, **Where r u? Can we talk?**

Typing again I answered, **With Elliot in city still. Talk tomorrow?**

I sat there looking at my phone waiting for it to beep again and was disappointed when it didn't. Elliot moved into my field of vision as he sat our breakfast dishes on the table.

"Everything ok?" he asked me for the second time that

morning.

"Yeah, everything's fine. Just David this time - saying sorry for ditching me last night." I moved back over to the table and sat down with Elliot, "This looks great." I told him, starting to dig in.

"I think I'll have to thank David for ditching you last night. I would have had to settle for dreaming about you last night instead of getting to spend time with the real thing."

I blushed a little, "You wouldn't have had to wait long. I was supposed to come to dinner tonight remember."

"I do remember," he said. "Do you still want to do that? Or do you have to get home?"

"I think I would still like to do that, if that's alright with you of course. Not sick of me yet?"

He leaned over and kissed me, "Um let me think - a beautiful woman who rocks my world and can talk sports with me; hmmm, no, I can't see myself getting sick of you any time soon." He had finished his eggs and took his plate to the sink leaning against it as he spoke to me, "I planned on going to the shops to get food for dinner tonight though if you don't mind coming along?"

"Sure, you wouldn't happen to have some women's clothes laying around would you? I don't really want to go out looking like I just stepped out of a club."

"I'll give you a shirt to wear over your dress if you like. Will that do?"

"That will be fine, thanks." I smiled, downing the last of my coffee. I stood up with my dishes and he moved towards me to take them, placing them in the sink.

He was a good ten centimetres taller than me in bare feet, and he leaned down to kiss me again, "But first, will you shower with me?"

I raised my eyebrows at him, and my eyes drifted to his chest. "You mean, I get to rub soap all over your body?" I asked tracing my fingers along the grooves between his muscles.

"I was thinking the same thing about you," he growled at me before he swooped me up and carried me laughing to the shower.

Chapter 14

We didn't end up making it out of the house to buy supplies for dinner, instead we spent the day exploring each other's bodies and minds – touching, tasting, whispering and, moaning together.

By the time our stomachs growled it was six o'clock, so we rummaged through his kitchen, deciding on fish finger sandwiches, topped off with a can of coke.

"I'm sorry this isn't a nicer dinner," he said to me as we ate quietly.

"Don't be," I nudged into him. "It's perfect." We locked eyes for a moment, completely engrossed by the pull our bodies seemed to emit around each other. He edged his chair closer to mine, lifting my leg so it was resting across his lap. With light fingertips, he ran his hand up and down it, giving me goose bumps all over.

"Will you stay again tonight?" he asked me in a husky voice.

"I would love to, you don't know how much I want to - but I should be getting home," I told him, registering the disappointment in his eyes. "I'm sorry. I just think my father would kill me if I came home tomorrow in the clothes I went out in on Friday night."

He nodded his understanding, "I'll drive you home after this then."

"I couldn't ask you to do that, it's too far. Just drop me off at the train station, I have to get my car anyway."

"Well then, I will drive you to your car," he insisted.

On the drive home something changed between us, the bubble we had been in while I was at his house had burst, and the real world had begun to seep through with its glaring reality.

For the next, I didn't know how long; I wasn't allowed to be openly affectionate with him. I wasn't allowed to touch him, to flirt with him, to give him meaningful looks. I felt a sense of loss as I sat there watching the scenery go by while the car brought us closer to the end of that perfect time together.

"You're very quiet," Elliot observed.

"Maybe I should just quit," I blurted out.

He glanced at me before setting his eyes back on the road, giving me a humourless smile, "Quit what? Work? I would never expect you to do that. Besides, it wouldn't matter, even if you did."

"What do you mean it wouldn't matter? If I'm not working there, then the 'no dating' policy shouldn't matter."

"I read over it; it says that you can't date a *recent* employee either. So it really doesn't matter." He glanced at me again and took my hand in his, resting them both on his leg as he drove. "We'll be ok. We just have to stay away from each other at the office so no one notices any change in our interactions." He glanced my way again, making sure I was in agreement. "Listen, how about, we skip drinks on Friday and go to my place instead?"

"What about your schmoozing time with the partners?"

"I think I can take one night off from that," he reasoned, giving my hand a light squeeze.

After agreeing to see him again the next Friday night, I felt more optimistic. A plan was in place so at the very least, we would continue our relationship. Although, I still couldn't help but feel that we'd never move beyond what we were at that point – a secret.

If I wasn't so hopelessly enamoured with Elliot, keeping things a secret probably wouldn't have bothered me. Normally, when I was apart from someone I was dating, it was kind of 'out of sight, out of mind' for me. With Elliot, it was different. Everything about him set my senses alive and since first meeting him, I had thought about him constantly. It was going to be a struggle for me to pretend there was nothing going on between us when all I ever wanted to do around Elliot, was jump into his arms.

I directed him to the back parking lot of Penrith Station and he pulled in next to my car, a white 1979 Mazda 323. The owner before me had installed central locking and put cow print seat covers inside it, which was what made me fall in love with it when I first saw it. I didn't even want to test drive it; I just wanted it. Luckily, it runs well and my father is a good mechanic, so he keeps it on the road for me.

I got out and checked it over, feeling relieved that nothing untoward had happened to it overnight.

"Cute car," Elliot commented, following me over.

"Thanks, she's my baby." I smiled, patting the roof as I leaned casually against the driver's door.

"So… Friday?" he asked, standing against me, his arms around my waist as he leaned in, brushing his lips against my own.

Parting my lips, I captured his mouth in mine, kissing him tenderly in farewell, feeling bittersweet in the knowledge that this would be our last chance for a whole week.

"Friday," I agreed, reluctantly getting into my car, putting an end to our all too brief encounter.

Instead of going straight home I decided to drive past David's house to see if his car was there, he still hadn't messaged me back, and I wanted to make sure he was ok.

Knocking twice, I stepped inside, finding his mother curled up on the couch, reading a book. "Hi Trina dear!" she greeted me, closing her book over her finger to momentarily mark her place, as I leaned down, giving her a cheek kiss. "You look lovely! Are you and David going out for a night on the town?"

I looked down at the dress I was still wearing from Friday. "No, not tonight," I told her. "I was just coming over to chat with

David. Is he in? I saw his car outside."

"Yes, he's in his room. Go right on through."

"Thanks Mrs Taylor."

She returned to her book as I walked down their narrow hallway to David's bedroom door. I tapped on it twice and opened it, revealing David lying on his bed, studying and listening to music with headphones on.

He smiled when he first saw me and set his work aside, sitting up as he removed the buds from his ears and switched his music off. As his eyes skittered across my dress, his smile disappeared and his face darkened.

"I see you haven't been home yet," he commented.

"No, I haven't. I was worried when you didn't message me back. I thought you might need to talk - more than I need to change my clothes."

"Everything's fine, Katrina. You worried yourself unnecessarily."

"Everything's not fine David. Where did you go last night? I looked everywhere for you."

Instead of answering me, he became defensive, "You can't have looked too hard for me. You were gone by the time I got back."

"We had missed *two* trains David! I looked for you and waited for over an hour!"

"I would never leave you on your own. I went back for you," he argued.

"How was I to know you were coming back? I couldn't find you David. You weren't answering your phone. You obviously weren't checking your messages, and I didn't want to catch the train on my own. Did you expect me to just hang around by myself?"

"Well you weren't on your own were you? Everyone told me you went off with that Connor guy and then the next day you tell me you were with Elliot. Doesn't sound very lonely to me Katrina."

"Why are you angry with me?" I asked incredulously.

"I'm not angry; I'm annoyed that you didn't trust that I would come back for you."

Huffing out my breath, I sat slumped, next to him on the bed.

"You still haven't told me where you were," I pointed out.

He looked down and brought his knee up to his chest taking on a defensive posture, "I was with Beth," he told me quietly.

My head buzzed with aggravation, I knew that was going to be his answer, and really, I had no right to be annoyed at him. Especially considering that I had slept with someone from my work too; but dammit, I was pissed.

"What is your fucking problem David?! Do you have to screw every girl you come across? I thought I asked you to leave the girls I work with alone!"

"You're such a fucking hypocrite Katrina! Who gives a shit if I screw a girl you work with? I'm not the one breaking any rules, running around in secret, and leading some Irish guy on because of it. Get the fuck over yourself Katrina, it was a screw. She knows it was nothing more than that."

"Does she? What about the next time, when you have moved on to, I don't know – Kayley, or Albina? What then? Do you think she will understand when she's watching that? Hell, I don't understand when I am watching that!"

"Well it bothers me watching you use some guy on the dance floor, and it bothers me that you went running off to fuck some guy that's going to cost you your job, leaving me to make *my* way home on my own - but that doesn't seem to bother you."

I opened my mouth to say something back, but I had nothing, we were just saying things to hurt each other and I wanted to go home.

Closing my eyes, I let out a shaky breath. "I'm sorry David," I said, my voice small as I stood under his stoic gaze and left his room, closing the door quietly behind me.

I don't really know which part I was sorry for – perhaps the situation as a whole; I just knew that when I left his room, I had lost any joy I had been feeling over the events of the past 24 hours.

Chapter 15

Back at work on Monday, I felt unlike myself. I still hadn't spoken to David after our argument on Saturday afternoon, and my time with Elliot was starting to feel more like a dream than a reality. When I did see him in the office, he didn't even look at me, adding to my sense of unease.

Normally spending Monday lunch with David, I was at a loss on my own. Grabbing a chicken salad wrap at the kiosk across the street, I went to sit outside, amongst the groups of people chatting around the water fountain in the Martin Place plaza. I had hoped that being around others would make me feel less lonely, but it only served to exacerbate my alienation.

Deep in thought, I threw pieces of flat bread to the pigeons milling about on the pavement for entertainment, until I saw Kayley waving and moving towards me.

"Well this isn't something I get to see every day – Katrina Roberts, sitting around on her lunch hour; Shouldn't you be off with David or running around a park somewhere?"

A hollow sound replaced my laugh, "Not today Kayley. I'm just doing my own thing this time."

Lowering herself to sit next to me, she asked, "Do you want to talk about it?"

Turning my head to meet her concerned and friendly face, I felt a sudden rush of emotion as my eyes threatened to spill my confusion out in the open. I blinked rapidly, concentrating on the pigeons to keep my control.

"I'm just all over the place Kayley, I'm supposed to be training for the selection races in January, and studying for my exams that are happening this week and next; but instead of focusing on those I am fighting with my best friend and attempting to have inappropriate relationships. It's all just a bit too much for me to deal with."

My phone chose that moment to beep, telling me I had a message. Hope swirled in my chest as I reached down, pulling it out of my pocket to read it, sighing in frustration upon seeing the name on the screen.

"Plus I keep getting these," I threw my hands in the air in annoyance.

"What? What is it?" I handed her my phone, showing her the text message I'd received. It read **Good luck in your exams, thinking of you. Love Christopher.**

"That's my ex. I get a call or a text from him at least once a week. Normally, I just ignore them, but right now they're bothering me - I have two men in my life that I desperately want to call or text, and the only one that does is the guy I don't want anything to do with!"

"Sounds like you have a lot going on right now," she said kindly, handing my phone back to me.

"When did my life become a soap opera? What happened to having fun, going out with friends and going to uni?"

"I don't know Katrina, but if you ever want to talk about things, I am happy to listen. No judgements, no repeating, just an ear to hear your troubles."

"Thanks Kayley, I appreciate that. You know, I think I am mainly upset not talking to David – it's not normal for us not to hang out or at least talk."

"Perhaps you should stop throwing your lunch at the birds and call him?" she suggested.

"Maybe… I might try calling him now actually," I got up decided that I'd rather call him from my desk instead of on a noisy city street, "I'll head back, you coming or staying out here a while longer?"

"I thought I'd go and grab a coffee across the street before I head back. Hope you sort things out with David."

Nodding, I gave her an appreciative smile as I left to walk back to my office's building. Standing just inside the entrance, I could see David, Beth and Bianca. I instantly stopped moving forward, taking a step to the side to watch the exchange unseen.

David was talking and laughing with them as Beth touched his arm flirtatiously. My breathing grew difficult and my heart leapt into my throat as I witnessed him lean in and kiss Beth goodbye before he started toward the door.

Not wanting to be spotted, I quickly turned and crossed the street to the coffee vendor where Kayley was lining up. I couldn't explain it but right at that moment I felt… betrayed. He was supposed to be my best friend, and here he was hanging out with the two people that made my working life more difficult. I guessed there was more to that night with Beth than just a screw then.

"I thought the coffee sounded like a great idea," I said with faked brightness as I approached Kayley, shooting a glance over her shoulder as David meandered down the street back to his work, my chest hurt, and I felt sick watching him.

Smiling, she offered to buy one for me, which I gratefully accepted, promising to get the next one. Taking our coffees upstairs I couldn't help giving Bianca the evil eye as I walked past reception and saw her talking and giggling with Beth.

She accepted my challenge saying, "Ever get the feeling that you're being replaced?"

Beth looked at me and giggled behind her hand. I stopped, venom dripping off my tongue and shot back, "Last I saw, it was you hanging off David, Bianca. Looks like you're the one he passed over."

"You know Katrina," Beth started, as she moved like a cat towards me, "David doesn't need you anymore, so you can run off with your little Irish boyfriends all you like now. He'll be fine with me."

I almost snorted, "David doesn't do relationships," I told her flatly.

"Oh, we'll see about that," Beth said boldly.

"Come inside, Katrina," Kayley urged me. "This isn't getting you anywhere."

I listened to her voice of reason and went back to the library, trying to immerse myself in work – I cursed that my job wasn't more complicated because my mind wouldn't stop thinking about why David would want to pursue either of those girls.

***

I was taking Wednesday off work for an exam, so I spent all of Tuesday studying and trying not to miss David too much. As we usually studied together, his absence was highly noted.

I picked up my phone a couple of times to call him but thought better of it - I didn't want to talk about seeing him with Beth and Bianca, and I especially didn't want him to confirm that he had started dating Beth; it was bad enough thinking it.

My brother Tom stuck his head inside my bedroom door to see if I wanted to walk up to the shops with him to get some fresh air. I agreed that I could use a break and put my shoes on.

"So how's your latest girlfriend? I never see you anymore," I enquired.

His face went all soft at the thought of her, and I could tell he really liked this girl, "She's great actually. I let her meet mum and dad on Saturday."

I was surprised; he had never brought a girl home before, "Wow, that's pretty epic for you. I'm sorry I missed it."

"That's ok. You were off with your latest anyway. You should have heard mum gushing about the guy you were with! Oh my god, I reckon if she was young enough, she'd go after him herself!" he laughed easily, "but seriously though - I'm glad you are moving on from that last guy. It's about time. You're young. You shouldn't be worried about dickheads like that... Is this one treating you nicely, or do I have to beat him up?"

It was my turn to laugh, "No, violence won't be necessary thanks. This guy, Elliot, is fine, he's nice. Things are just complicated because we work together, that's all."

"Complicated huh?" I nodded, not wanting to elaborate, "I couldn't help but notice the absence of David today. Is something going on with you two? You seem pretty mopey for a girl in a new relationship. Aren't you supposed to be running through fields of wild flowers right now, sighing all the time?"

"Yeah, well David and I got into a bit of a fight on Saturday night before I came home," I filled him in on most of the details and explained why I dislike him spending time Beth and Bianca.

"Do you think maybe you're jealous?"

"No Tom, I don't think I'm jealous – I think I'm pissed off," I said incredulously.

"Hey relax, I'm just checking. He's normally a bit of a wombat with girls, and now he's actually hanging out with one, and she's not you. I thought that might bring out the green-eyed monster a bit."

"What the hell does a wombat have to do with it?" I asked, not understanding his analogy.

"You know, a wombat – eats, roots and leaves."

I chuckled, "I haven't heard that one before."

"Well, you can have that one – keep it in your pocket and use it for later; I've got loads," he joked with me.

"How very generous of you," I said sarcastically.

"Hey, what are big brothers for?"

***

I stood outside the exam room waiting to go inside, looking around, hoping to find David. Although, I couldn't see him anywhere. Despite feeling hurt by him, I was missing him terribly; this was the longest we had ever gone without talking or seeing each other since we met as kids.

My phone beeped, **Good luck in your exam, will miss you at lunch. Evan :P**

I smiled to myself at the use of his alter ego, tapped out a thanks and put my phone to silent.

I didn't spot David until we were inside ready to take the exam. We were allowed to leave after the first hour but had three hours to complete the booklet.

When the examiner announced the hour was up, a few people got up to walk out, one of them being David. Seeing him leave gave me cause to scramble and get my things together, handing my exam in unfinished to go after him.

Rushing, I caught him just outside the building, as he headed in the direction of the parking lot. "David!" I yelled out.

He stopped and looked up to the sky as if he couldn't believe I was coming after him. He didn't turn to look at me; he just stood there until I reached him.

"What do you want Katrina?" he asked flatly.

"I want to talk to you! Why are you being like this?" I demanded.

"Because I'm pissed off at you Katrina! I thought that was all pretty clear from Saturday."

"Are you serious? You're going to hold the fact that I didn't wait for you against me?! How long for?"

"Lower your voice Katrina, you're causing a scene," he warned me through gritted teeth.

"I don't care!" I yelled.

"You want to do this here do you? Fine, we'll do it here - I am glad that you feel ready to date again Katrina. I really am. But I'm not going to stand by while you fall head over heels for some muscle-bound guy who treats you like shit because it's all a secret. Did you know he has been with Beth too? Kept it all a secret so nobody knew anything, just like what he is doing with you."

"That's not true. I'm the only …"

"How do you know that? Because he told you? Maybe that's just what he does; maybe he has a whole string of secret girlfriends. Have you considered that?" He stood glaring at me, and I opened and closed my mouth, not knowing how to respond.

"You know what Katrina, you can do whatever you want – I won't stand in your way. But I will be damned if I will stand by and watch you fawn all over him, while I cop the brunt of your boyfriend's insecurities again – I won't do it – not this time!"

"So what? I'm not supposed to date anyone now? Or I just can't date unless you approve of them?"

"You're supposed to be careful, date openly – date guys who are cool with you being around me. I'm just sick of this shit!" He threw his hands up and started to walk away from me.

"Stop David," I ran to move in front of him, "Where the hell is all this coming from? Did Elliot say something to you?"

He stopped again, "He doesn't have to say anything, it's all over his face when he sees me near you. Every guy you've ever dated has a problem with me. When it's just you and me, we have a great time – we don't work with when there's another guy around; I never expect you to hang out with the girls I am seeing!" he argued.

"That's because you only fuck David, you don't *see* anybody.

How many times have I had to sit by and watch you flirt and pick up every girl around us? Do you think that's fun for me? Do you think I actually want you fucking around with the girls I work with? No, I don't! But you can't seem to keep your dick in your pants, so who gives a fuck about what Katrina wants!" I narrowed my eyes at him as I watched his face screw up with hurt and anger from my words.

"I have never left you somewhere to go and screw some girl. If I am with you – I am with you. But every time we go out with people from your work you go off flirting and leave me on my own, what am I supposed to do? Just stand there and watch you make a fool of yourself? There has to be something in it for me too besides being your fall-back guy, Katrina."

I stood with my hands on my hips as I considered what he said, "What are you talking about? You left me to go and screw Beth on Friday!" I countered, watching him as he shifted on his feet before I went on, "Besides that, you think you're my fall-back guy? You think that's what you are to me?"

He looked at the ground, scowling, "Maybe."

I shook my head, "Goes to show how little you think of me." We stood for a moment, looking everywhere but at each other as we gathered our thoughts.

Taking a calming breath, I ploughed ahead, "I saw you with Beth...Are you dating now?" I had to ask, even though I didn't really want the answer.

"I guess," he mumbled with a shrug of his shoulders.

"Are you with her to spite me?"

He held his hands out to the sides as his irritation flared, "Maybe I like her Katrina, have you ever considered that?" he glared at me, waiting for my response.

No, I hadn't considered that. Why Beth? Why now? I felt that the only possible reason for him to be dating her was to hurt me somehow. I couldn't understand why he'd want to do that.

"So I guess it's true - you don't need me anymore," I ventured.

"What the fuck is that supposed to mean?"

"Beth told me that you don't need me anymore," I told him, tears brimming in my eyes.

David's face scrunched up as he responded, "That's bullshit Katrina! Why would she even say that?!"

"I don't know David – why did she say she slept with Elliot?"

"Probably because he's fucking around with every girl in the office and whole bloody lot of you are stupid enough to think you're the only one!" he bit out in retort.

I stood there open mouthed looking at my best friend, my only real friend and all I could see was anger and what looked like hatred in his face. A face that had shown me nothing but kindness before now, it broke my heart to see him look at me this way.

My voice was small and quiet when I spoke, "I can't do this anymore. Why are you trying to hurt me?" I glared at him, pained and confused. "I just want my friend back, David. I miss you – I miss us; this… this fighting – it isn't how we treat each other… I just want things to go back to the way they were."

He ran his hands through his hair and blew out a breath that was charged with his emotions, "I can't do this anymore either. I can't watch you get hurt again, Katrina. I'm sorry," he finished and started walking away from me once more.

I wanted to call after him to tell him I wouldn't get hurt again, that he didn't need to worry. I wanted to beg him to stay with me and tell him that I needed him, that I didn't know who I was without him. Instead, I just stood there watching as my friend walked away from me while silent tears rolled down my face.

Chapter 16

Standing in front of Elliot, stretching as he ran on the treadmill at lunch time that Friday, I blurted out, "I fucked up my exam on Wednesday."

He raised his eyebrows, "What makes you think that?"

"I left before I was finished," I told him flatly.

He looked surprised, "Why would you do that?"

"I needed to talk to David," I watched for his expression to change; it just looked curious, not at all jealous like I was expecting.

"You couldn't wait to talk to him until after your exam?"

"In hindsight of course I could have waited, but at the time I wasn't really thinking."

"So… what was so important?"

"He's not speaking to me right now; It's killing me because we haven't gone more than a day or two without talking since we were kids."

"And did you find out why he isn't speaking to you?"

"He thinks that after what happened with Christopher, I shouldn't be dating secretly."

"Does he think I'm like Christopher?" he looked concerned as he started to slow the machine down so he could hop off.

"No, I don't think so, he was kind of all over the place when we were arguing. He said that he was tired of the guys I date being jealous of him, and that he was tired of watching me get hurt. And he told me something that Beth told him... about you."

He raised his eyebrows in question, "What did she tell him?" Finished on the treadmill, he moved in front of me, hands on his hips as he listened.

I looked out of the window, not really wanting to meet his eyes, afraid that it might be true, "That you slept with her too – in secret; just like you are doing with me."

When I looked at him his eyes were wide in astonishment,

"And you believe that?"

"No… well, not at first. I guess it doesn't really matter, but… I do feel like I need to know."

He looked me in the eye as he spoke, "I have never slept with her Katrina. I thought I'd made that clear. I have at no time been interested in her," he told me sincerely, "and just for the record, Katrina, I'm not jealous of David, and I am not planning on hurting you. Ok?"

I nodded, "I'm sorry I just had to ask."

"It's fine, I'll deal with Beth. Maybe just give David a little time to get used to us," he suggested.

He put a reassuring hand on my shoulder, my body reacting instantly to his touch, screaming to have more of him. "I've missed you this week," I told him honestly.

He gave me one of his brilliant smiles and I swooned. "Me too," he whispered.

***

I was first to arrive outside the parking garage were Elliot parked his car. Standing by the entrance, holding my gym bag that also held some clean clothes for tomorrow, I waited almost five minutes before I saw him coming down the street towards me.

Looking at him and seeing him smile at the sight of me made all the worries I had been having over the past week disappear, I was once again getting trapped in the cocoon of having him all to myself. He swept me up in his arms and spun me around laughing, before he put me down and kissed me tenderly with his hands cupped either side of my face.

I kept my eyes closed and breathed, "Finally."

He chuckled softly, "Do you know how hard it is for me not to touch you or kiss you whenever I see you around the office? I have been in agony." He kissed me again and we both moaned into each other's mouths, softly tasting each other, getting lost in each other, numbing the sound of the city street beside us.

He broke the kiss and grabbed my hand, interlacing our fingers, "Come on."

I spotted his car up ahead, a navy blue SAAB sedan. Reading the badges on the back as we approached, I noted a '95' on one side and 'turbo 4' on the other – I had no idea what that meant but judging from the dark grey leather interior and how smooth the ride home was last week; I knew it had to be expensive.

"I didn't actually pay attention to your car last week. It's nice." I told him as we got in.

"Thanks, but my dad owns it – there's no way I could buy this on my salary," he disclosed.

"Your Dad bought it for you?"

"No, he owns it. He bought it for me to use, but I don't own anything – his way of keeping me in line I guess."

"So let me get this straight – your dad owns the flat you live in, buys you a car and pays your living expenses? To me, that's a pretty sweet deal."

"I suppose, but everything comes at a price. My price is that my father feels that he can control me."

I was thoughtful for a moment, "So why do you let him then? Pay for everything, I mean."

He kept his eyes on the road as he spoke, easily navigating the city streets, "I guess I like not having to worry about money – there's no way I could afford to live in Bondi on my own, and as long as I work hard he's happy to support me."

He had the radio station tuned to Triple M. The music ended and a comedy duo hosting were talking about playing rugby naked.

We both listened, laughing at their antics until the station started to run advertisements before the six o'clock news. "I made a pot of bolognaise sauce for us for tonight, are you happy with spaghetti for dinner?"

"I love spaghetti. You made a great choice."

"Well, it wasn't much of a choice. I can do steak, and I can do pasta. I'm not the greatest chef in the world."

He glanced and me and we smiled at each other, wanting to be together physically more than we wanted to make small talk while driving.

"How about you, can you cook anything?" he asked me.

"Sure, if it comes out of a box and goes directly in the oven."

He responded with an amused sound before he reached for my hand and placed it on his lap, as he did the last time we drove together. My fingers were itching to make their way further across his lap to feel him as he drove.

I took a deep breath for courage. I wasn't normally a big

initiator where sex was concerned, but I couldn't seem to stop myself. I slid my hand up his thigh, stopping as my hand brushed his bulge, ever so lightly. I heard him suck in his breath softly, anticipating my touch but keeping his eyes steady on the road.

Becoming bolder, I moved my hand further until I felt his now hard shaft, straining through his pants, I curled my fingers around it and moved my hand up and down the fabric, delighting as I felt him get harder, hearing his breathing change to those charged careful breaths that come with arousal.

He started to moan lightly, fighting to keep his focus. I could feel my juices beginning to flow as I watched the way his body reacted to me and imagined what it would be like to take him in my mouth.

Suddenly, he clamped his hand down on mine. "Wait! We're almost there," he told me as we turned into his street, and he parked the car.

We practically ran up the stairs to get inside his flat, needing desperately to be on our own. The moment he opened the door, I threw my bag down and pushed him up against the wall, smiling wickedly. Kissing him fervently, I slid my hand down his chest and further, until I was cupping his erection.

He moaned as I stroked him, before he forcefully pushed me back so I was the one pinned against the wall. With a cocky half grin, he kissed me back, his arms either side of me, caging me between the wall and his body. Anxiously, I pulled at his belt, undoing it before sliding it loose and dropping on the floor next to us. Using deft fingers, I undid his button and zip, hooking the waistband of both his pants and underwear to drag them with me as I slid my body down the wall, freeing his erection. I slid my hands up under his shirt to feel his smooth hard chest like satin beneath my hands, and brought my tongue out to tease his tip, tasting the saltiness of his arousal before sliding my hands back down to grasp him and take him into the wetness of my mouth.

He shuddered as I swirled my tongue around his nob, gently rubbing my teeth over his ridge. His shudder became a moan as I took him as deeply into my mouth as I could, shafting him with my hand and sucking with my mouth at the same time.

With his hands still against the wall he moaned and whispered to me, becoming more urgent with his sounds. I took his balls into my other hand and gently squeezed, sucking him firmly into my mouth. As he moaned out my name, I felt his hot juices pour into my mouth. I sucked and swallowed, milking him of every last drop.

Strong arms reached down and hauled me up the wall, where he kissed me zealously. Wildly, he lifted my skirt and pulled my panties down my legs, flicking them aside like wrapping paper from a gift, before he ran his fingers in between my folds, groaning as he slid back and forth.

"You are so wet," he whispered into my open mouth.

I gasped out, whimpering as he pushed his fingers inside me rubbing against my inner wall and using his thumb to rub over my clit. A glorious sensation filled my body as my orgasm rocked through me suddenly. Calling out with intensity, I writhed against his hand, clamping my legs together to still his movement when the sensation became too much.

"Relax," he murmured.

Parting my thighs, I released his hand, feeling him slide it down my leg to behind my knee where he lifted my leg, guiding it around his waist. Our heights gave him the perfect access, and he pushed his erection forward into me, pumping into me against the wall. I continued to call out as I rode the still present waves of my orgasm, clenching myself tightly around him.

"Oh my god – you're like a vice," he shuddered, breathing carefully as he came deep inside me.

Heaving against each other we kissed, a long slow, steady kiss.

"A week without being with you is far too long," he gasped out.

We stayed connected as we tried to look for something within reach to try to catch the mess that was about to fall out of me. "Looks like we're stuck like this," I said intimately.

"I'll catch it," he offered softly, as he pulled out and cupped his hand at my opening, collecting his come as it spilled from inside me. Staring into my eyes, he started to swirl his thumb gently around my clit, my mouth fell open as I started to lose focus, becoming drowned in an all new arousal.

"That should do it," he said as he gently pulled away from me, leaving me wanting him even more.

I laughed as he awkwardly tried to shuck his shoes and kick his pants aside so he could go to the bathroom and clean his hand. Standing there, an amused half grin on my face, I watched him walk down the hallway in just his work shirt and a pair of socks.

Chapter 17

"I have to go home this morning," I said quietly, stroking the hair on Elliot's head as he lay on my naked chest, listening to my heartbeat after night filled with exploring each other's bodies and very little sleep.

He lifted his head to look at me, "Can't you stay tonight as well?" he asked earnestly.

"I can't. I have a session with my swimming coach this afternoon, plus I have an exam to study for."

"Is that the last of your exams?"

I sighed, "Yes, thank goodness. Then no more uni until February next year."

"Good, then we can celebrate. How about I take you out next Saturday night? Bring your stuff on Friday and stay here for the weekend. I'll take you home Sunday afternoon."

"I'd like that," I told him, playing with his hair so it was sticking up. I reached down and then dragged my nails up his back, causing shivers to run down his spine. He hummed his contentment, griping when I stopped and tapped him on the shoulder, asking him to hop up.

He groaned unhappily as he rolled off me, "We don't get enough time!" he complained.

"We'll get more time next weekend," I said as I stood up and gathered my toiletries bag, "I need to shower, will you drive me to the station after breakfast?"

"I'll drive you to your car again," he told me.

"Elliot, it's too much petrol; I am fine on the train."

"No, I'm not just fucking you and dumping you at the train station. This is supposed to be a relationship. I want to drive you; I want to spend a bit more time with my girlfriend," he said indignantly.

"Alright, you can drive me," I soothed, trying not to react to being called his girlfriend; a smile played at the edge of my lips none the less.

I turned and walked into the bathroom, turning on the shower to wait for it to warm up.

"Do you want me to wash your back?" he called from the bedroom.

"No thank you. I'll never get home if we start that again!" I called back teasingly.

 "That's the point," he said, appearing at the door, reaching out and pulling me towards him.

***

Two hours later we were on the road back to Penrith. I didn't feel as though our bubble was bursting this time, we talked comfortably with each other, touching when we could and making plans to continue training together at lunch times so we could still see each other during the week. Now that David wasn't having lunch with me; Mondays could be used for training as well.

"Aren't you worried that someone will see us training together and figure something is up?" I asked him.

"No," he said simply.

"Why not? Someone could see us outside the office, and not just training – they could see us, like, now; in the car together or they could have seen us outside the parking garage on Friday."

"Katrina, the only people we have to worry about are the gossips of the office, and they're too busy on Friday nights drinking and, well, gossiping – and the same goes for lunch times. Besides, there's no rule that says we can't be seen together, we just can't be seen to be dating. So don't worry, if Andrew and Carmen can wander around holding hands the moment they step out of the office, I think we can safely train together and kiss in a parking garage."

"Yes, but Andrew isn't you."

"What's that supposed to mean?" he asked looking genuinely confused.

"Jesus, Elliot, look in the mirror! The women at the office salivate over you."

He let out a small chuckle, "I don't think it's that bad."

"You're not the one who copped the evil eyes when we were busted on the wharf. Believe me, you could snap your fingers at any woman in that office, and they'd undress for you."

He shuddered like his skin was crawling, "Uh, don't say that -

there's some pretty scary ladies in that office."

I took that as a challenge and started filling his mind with images of some of the less desirable women waiting for him around corners and throwing themselves at him.

"Great, now I'm going to have nightmares," he said half teasingly as he pulled up in a parking space close to my car.

"Well, I can't leave you like that," I said seductively, as I climbed over the centre console and onto his lap.

"What are you doing?" he asked, a slight nervous edge to his voice.

"Altering your dream," I murmured, capturing his mouth in mine, kissing him fervidly, my fingers entwined in his hair as I pulled him closer.

Rocking my hips so we were rubbing up against each other, I could feel his arousal pressing solidly against my own. He moaned and reached down to slide the seat back, giving us more room.

He started to brush soft kisses down my neck and across my chest, massaging my breasts with his hands through my clothes. He rocked his hips up and pressed his erection firmly between my legs, "Oh god, do you see what you do to me? I don't think I can let you out of this car," he growled.

I smiled mischievously at him as I reached down to release him from the confines of his pants, pulling my panties to the side to take his length inside me. We both let out a long steady breath as I lowered myself over him, locking eyes while I slowly moved in his lap.

We moved carefully together, luxuriating in our continued closeness and watching as our own desire was mirrored in the others face. When he came I clenched my muscles against his spasms and kept on moving, knowing my own orgasm was ready to explode at any moment. As I erupted I pulled his head to my chest and held him tightly, while he held my hips down and pushed us together as deeply as we could manage. It was as if we were trying to meld together somehow.

Letting out a calming breath he murmured, "So I guess you're not worried about anyone from work seeing us here then."

I laughed through my nose and kissed him, "No, not at all."

I reached into my handbag for some tissues to put between my legs so we could separate and moved back into the passenger seat.

He looked around for a moment and rested his head back in his chair, watching me closely, a bewildered expression on his face.

"What?" I asked.

He shook his head slightly, "It's just you, you get me doing things I wouldn't normally do."

I shrugged modestly, "It's a god given talent," I opened the door and got out, turning to him before I closed it, "I'll see you Monday."

He nodded, giving me a smouldering look that made me want to jump back into his lap again. It took some will power but I got into my car and waved my goodbye as I started to drive home, slipping out of the bubble that encapsulated us when we were together.

***

When I walked through the door, I was greeted by silence, my parents had obviously gone out, most likely to have lunch together, and my brother was, god only knows where. I dropped my bag on the floor in my room and flopped down on to my bed, exhausted after not sleeping much last night.

I was woken by the sound of the doorbell a couple of hours later. As I trudged to the door half asleep, the person waiting started knocking insistently. "I'm coming!" I called out, feeling irritated.

Looking through the peephole, I could see David standing on the porch, "Come on Katrina, let me in. I can hear you breathing on the other side of the door."

I was both excited and nervous when I opened it, "Are you going to have a go at me again?" I asked him trepidatiously.

He laughed through his nose and shook his head, "No, I just want to talk to you," he said, and I stepped aside to allow him through.

I led him to the family room, where we sat facing each other on the couch, "So… what do you want to talk about?" I asked, searching his face for his current state of mind.

He gave little away, "I just had a very interesting conversation," he started.

When he didn't continue I urged, "and?"

"Elliot came to visit me."

"He what?"

"He said he got my number from Carmen - he called me and asked if he could come and have a chat with me."

I sat watching his handsome face struggle with something before he spoke again, "I want to say I'm sorry Katrina. He's not as bad as I thought he was."

"What? That's all you're going to tell me - what did you talk about, what did he say?"

"All we talked about was you and how important you are to both of us. I guess we kind of have… an understanding now."

"Did he tell you he hasn't slept with Beth?"

"Yes he did."

"Did you believe him?"

"I did."

"Ok, well – where does this leave us?" I asked hopefully.

"I don't know Katrina."

"But…I need you David. You're my best friend," it came out almost as a hoarse whisper, laced with tears that were threatening to spill from my eyes as I feared the worst.

He sighed and took my hand in his, and spoke to it instead of me. "When Christopher hurt you, it made me realise how… important, you were to me – are to me. I just didn't realise that seeing you move on from him would be this hard to handle. I know I'm being selfish, but I don't think I can handle you dating anymore Katrina. It's like I'm petrified something is going to happen to you again, and I'm not going to be able to stop it this time. That thought; it makes me so angry. And while I'm angry, I'm not worried. Either way I feel horrible whenever I see or think about you with him, with anyone - and I don't know what to do about it."

"I don't understand, are you saying we can't go back to being friends like we were only a week ago? I miss you David. I'm lonely without you!" I could feel myself shaking, so scared that whatever was happening between us couldn't be fixed.

"Listen, I'm glad that you're with someone like Elliot. He really does seem like a decent guy. But, I'm struggling here Trina. It's hard for me to be around you."

"David – what is this? I feel like you're breaking up with me," tears were now brimming in my eyes, and it was taking all of my self-control not to let them spill out.

"I just need time to sort out my head Katrina," he told me as he stood up, releasing my hand. He leaned down and kissed the top of my head, "We're still friends. It's just different now - that's all." With that, he left, once again taking my happiness with him.

***

"How are things with Elliot?" my mother asked me as I helped her put the groceries she had come home with away.

"They're pretty great. It's wonderful when we're together, and we get along so well - " I let the sentence hang in the air.

"But?" my mother prompted me.

"But everything else in my life seems to be turning to shit as a consequence." My mother looked at me, patiently waiting. She had been making such and effort not to ask too many questions lately, and it had really improved our relationship.

It had improved so much that I poured my heart out to her and shared all of my troubles, something I hadn't done in a long time. I told her about David's reaction to me and Elliot, and the fact that he seemed to be dating one of the two bitchiest women from my office, and I told her the way they treated me when David wasn't around.

"I can see what you mean," my mother said as I finished, "I suppose the thing with you, and Christopher was really hard on David, so I can understand he's upset. I just don't understand why he is letting it affect your friendship so much.

"Is there something about Elliot that you're not telling me? Is that why David is so upset?"

"No mum, Elliot is a good guy – David even said so himself."

"Unless - " my mother said thoughtfully.

"Unless what, mum?"

She shook her head, "Oh nothing. I'm sure it will all work out in the end."

"I hope so mum, because I hate not talking to him and seeing him all the time. It just feels so – wrong – when he's not around, you know?"

My mum gave me a tight hug and assured me that things would get better in time. I thanked her for listening to me and went into my room to study for the exam I had on Thursday for one of my humanities subjects. David wouldn't be there this time, so I would actually manage to complete this one.

***

I wasn't at work for long on Monday morning when my internal line rang. I answered it with my usual greeting, smiling when I heard Elliot's voice rumble down the line.

"I need you to hear something," he said to me.

"Ok, what is it?" I asked intrigued.

"Just give me a minute, I'm going to set the phone down. Ok?"

"Ok…" I could hear the clunk of the receiver as he put it down on his desk as well as the movement of his chair.

I was wondering what he could possibly want me to hear when he said, "Beth, can I see you in my office please?"

I held my breath as I heard him take his seat and tell Beth to take a seat as well.

"What can I do for you Elliot?" she asked politely.

He cleared his throat, "Beth, it's been brought to my attention that you may have been exaggerating your relationship with me."

His statement was met with silence, and I could only imagine the look on Beth's face.

"Allegations like that could cost me my job Beth. Now you and I both know that I have been nothing but professional with you. So I would appreciate it if you would set these rumours straight before they get out of hand."

Beth immediately started stammering, "Elliot, I-I-I don't know w-what you heard, b-but I would never try to cause you any problems. I will make sure whoever is spreading rumours knows that they're false."

"Thank you Beth, you can go now."

I heard her get up and leave his office, and the click of the door behind her. Elliot then picked up the receiver to speak to me again.

"Did you get all that?" he asked me.

"Yes, I did. But you didn't have to do that – I believed you when you said nothing happened."

"I did need to do that. The rumour needs to be stopped before it goes any further. Plus, I wanted to make sure there was no doubt in your mind."

"There wasn't, I trust you," I said sincerely. "I'll see you at lunch?"

"See you then."

I met Elliot at the sign I was reading the first time we ran together. It was now our usual meeting spot inside the botanical gardens.

As we started running I had to talk about something that had been playing on my mind, "Elliot," I started. "Why did you go and visit David?"

He looked at me to gauge my mood before he answered, "You were upset, and I wanted to try to help things a bit by letting him know that I wasn't planning on challenging your friendship with him. Do you mind that I spoke to him?" he asked with raised eyebrows.

"No, not really. It's actually kind of nice that you did." In truth, it was. Elliot was the first guy I had dated, that actually tried to work things out with David instead of fighting it. It was just a pity that David didn't seem so willing this time around.

We ran along in quiet for a moment before Elliot said, "Did it help at all?"

"Yes and no, he is talking to me again but not like he was

before."

"I'm sorry to hear that, I thought he might be ok now."

"I think the stuff with Christopher just messed with his head a bit too much. He'll come around in time – or so my mum says anyway."

"She's probably right."

"I hope so… So, why *don't* you have a problem with David? I only ask because every other guy I have dated has a *huge* problem with him."

"At first, I'll admit, I was a bit worried about him. Especially seeing how close you two were, but then I thought about how I'd feel if David was a woman and it was just your typical best friends situation, it was then that I realised I had no reason to be jealous."

"That's the way I always thought about it," I told him.

Chapter 18

With my exams finally over I was looking forward to spending the weekend with Elliot and not worrying about having to go home to study or train, it was a weekend off everything, and I was bursting with excitement.

I was heading down to the parking garage when I ran into David, we hadn't spoken since the weekend, but we had been exchanging texts. So things were improving, which is better than the radio silence I was getting from him before.

"Hi," I said to him as brightly as I could, "are you going up to meet Beth?" I tried to keep my voice friendly, even though I really disliked that he was dating her and I hated that our friendship was so strained.

"Yeah, we're going out to celebrate the end of exams," he told me, not really making eye contact. "You're not staying for drinks?"

I shrugged. "No, not this time. Have fun though," I said, feeling awkward. We stood there looking at each other, trying to overcome the tension that was between us. I desperately wanted to hug him and tell him how much I missed him, but I knew that wasn't going to help anything right now. I gave him a tight smile and nodded. "See you around, David," I hitched my overnight bag higher on my shoulder and left the building, giving him a small wave as I walked past the glass exterior and saw him watching me as he waited for the lift.

The parking garage was about a ten-minute walk away. Elliot had texted me that he was on his way down before I left so I was expecting to see him waiting outside the entrance.

"Hey stranger," he said to me as I got close enough, holding the door open and ushering me through. He took my bag and caught my hand as soon as it clicked shut.

"Thank you," I said leaning into him, it was so wonderful to be able to touch him again after spending a week near him with nothing more than stolen glance here and there. It made it all the more important to be in as much physical contact with each other when we could.

"I was thinking we could eat Chinese for dinner," he told me casually.

I couldn't help myself, "I'm not much of a cannibal Elliot, but if that's what you're into – I'm not going to stop you," I replied jokingly. Elliot was shaking his head and smiling his amusement at my good-natured jibe.

"I thought we might get some take away Chinese *food* for dinner."

"Oh Chinese *food*! I love Chinese food - that would be amazing. I'm starving!"

Elliot dragged my head towards him and kissed me roughly in my hair, I looked at him wondering what that was for and he told me, "Because you're funny."

We stopped at his car, and he opened the boot to put my bag inside. Pulling me to him, he kissed me passionately. "Mmm perhaps I should just have you for dinner," he murmured as we parted.

"Is it as hard for you as it is for me – the weeks between?" I asked as we got into the car and started on our way.

"I think it's harder," he said looking at me hungrily; it sent shivers through me as my own world fell away and I became Elliot focused once more.

We drove straight to Elliot's flat, not bothering with small talk but instead just luxuriating in the sexual tension that was filling the air between us, arousing and intoxicating. Racing up the stairs to his door, we didn't even realise that we had left my bag in the boot of his car, our need for each other was too over powering to care about trivial things like clean clothes.

As soon as the locks clicked he turned and took my face in his hands and kissed me, breathing me in as he did so, making me feel as if I was melting into his body. He took me by the hand and led me straight to his bedroom, kissing me again as he slowly undid the buttons of my blouse to slide his hands over my bare skin.

Everywhere his hands had been screamed for more as his touch moved on, my body was craving him like he was the sustenance that kept me living. He let my blouse drop to the floor as he guided me over to the bed, unzipping my skirt and sliding it down my legs as he urged me to lay back, propping a pillow under my hips as he removed my panties and positioned himself between my legs.

"It seems a little unfair that you still have your clothes on," I spoke, my voice husky with desire.

"You're still wearing your bra," he murmured wickedly, as he started kissing a trail across my stomach, while he teased my opening with his finger. He groaned, "I love that you're always so wet for me."

With his finger, he slid my juices up towards my clit. I let out a slight gasp as he began to circle it. Around him, it seemed to always be throbbing; a result of the desire I continuously felt when in his presence.

He kissed a trail down my stomach and over my mound, flicking his tongue over my swollen clit and sucking it as he slid his fingers back towards my opening until they were inside me. I moaned, clenching myself tightly around his fingers, "Oh, it's so hot when you do that," he let out.

Returning to tease my clit with his tongue, his fingers continued to massage my depths. There was little warning as my orgasm ripped through me, sudden and explosive. He withdrew his fingers and held onto me tightly while my hips spasmed and he continued to lap at my folds. When I screamed out enough, he released me, wiping his mouth as he sat back on his haunches. Prepared to continue our sexual encounter, I was surprised when he stood up and offered me his hand.

"Let's go and order something for dinner," he suggested, pulling me up off the bed towards him.

"What about you?" I asked, boldly running my fingers over the erection straining the zipper of his pants. He closed his eyes for a moment and caught my hand, kissing me softly.

"What about me?" He had a look of mischief about him as he backed out of the room, leaving me standing there with just my bra on and wanting him badly. I took my bra off and grabbed a shirt from over the back of a chair and dropped it over my head, following him out. I lifted the shirt to my nose and breathed in his scent, which to me was everything I found erotic.

I found him in the kitchen pulling take away menus out of a drawer; he smiled appraisingly at me as he took in my clothing choice.

"That's now my favourite shirt," he said, taking me in his arms and kissing me, hooking his finger in the neck of the shirt and pulling it towards him to look inside. He saw that I was completely naked underneath and raised his eyebrows at me, snaking his other hand down from my waist to slide under the shirt and caress my bare behind. "My absolute favourite shirt," I melted into his hard chest once more as we kissed again, his hands roaming over my body underneath the shirt.

In a show of great restraint, he stepped away and said, "What would you like to order?"

"Elliot, with a side of more Elliot," I purred reaching for the button of his pants and undoing it. He caught my hand again.

"Soon," he told me, kissing my nose and guiding me, so I was sitting on a chair - pouting. "Is satay and fried rice fine with you?"

I nodded and listened as he called the restaurant, asking for home delivery.

"It's going to be about an hour," he informed me when he was finished.

"Well, what are we going to do with all that time?"

He moved towards me, lifted me from my chair and sat me on the table, taking the seat in front of me. "This," he told me as he leaned forward and slid his tongue into my folds for the second time in less than half an hour. I was still sensitive from coming the first time, so he was careful not to press his tongue too firmly on my clit. He used soft gentle laps to ease me into the build-up of another orgasm. I moaned out my pleasure as his mouth and fingers teased me until I was once again writhing in ecstasy while his mouth drank me in.

This time he followed through, undoing his pants as he stood, ramming his cock inside me causing me to gasp from the suddenness of it. I clutched myself against him and breathed into his ear, "Yes. That's what I needed – you inside me."

He pushed deeply into me and lifted me from the table, walking with us still connected until he was sitting on the couch, and I was on top of him, grinding my hips, so I could take in every millimetre of his length.

He held me tightly to him and pushed back, touching me deeply. When he let go, I lifted myself up until he was just about to slide out of me before I slid back down again, griping him tightly as I repeated the process. He threw his head back and moaned, his hands resting on my hips as he guided my rhythm.

His body shuddered and he held his breath as he came, burying his face in my neck and kissing me. I curled my fingers through his hair and tilted his head up, so I could kiss him back, wriggling in his lap to enjoy our continued connection.

The intercom buzzed with what I assumed would be our dinner delivery, "I'll catch it this time," I said to him.

"You don't have to, I'm prepared," he told me as he nodded

towards a box of tissues on the coffee table in front of us.

Grinning, I reached for them, "Well done," I praised, impressed. I slid off him and used the tissues to clean myself while he did his pants up and went to answer the intercom.

I could hear Elliot talking to the delivery guy at the front door and went into the kitchen, threw the tissues in with the rubbish, washed my hands and pulled two plates out of the strainer next to the sink to set the table.

I turned as I heard the rustle from the plastic bag Elliot was carrying, "I hope you're hungry," he stated, holding up the take-away containers. He placed the bag on the table, and I started to unpack it, opening each container and setting it on the table in front of our plates. He moved over to the drawer and took out forks and spoons for us, setting them on the table also. He then went to the fridge and poked his head inside. "Beer, wine or coke?" he offered.

"Hmmm, wine I think – is it white? If not, then beer."

"Yeah it's white," he told me taking out the bottle and getting two glasses and a corkscrew from the cupboard above his head before he poured us both a glass.

"Here's to a full weekend together and the end of your exams," he toasted me, clinking our glasses together and looking me straight in the eye. I could lose myself in those eyes of his, like gleaming deep blue beacons, shining in a sea of white.

I reached out and touched his face as I sipped my drink, feeling the rough of his stubble starting to edge out of his skin. He turned his head to kiss my hand, smiling at me like it was the most natural thing in the world for us to be together. If it wasn't for what the world was like outside these walls, I would think that it was too, we seemed inexplicably drawn together.

"I wish I had have gotten a job at a different law firm," I said suddenly to him.

"Why? You regretting meeting me?" he teased.

"Of course not, besides - we still would have met; you would have seen me running in the park and felt compelled to start talking to me," I smiled batting my eyelashes comically at him.

He raised his eyebrows thoughtfully, "You know. I don't know if I would have been that audacious if I didn't know you from the office," he told me truthfully.

"Really?" The revelation surprised me. "Well, I would have found a way to talk to you," I reasoned.

"I'd hope so," he picked up a spring roll and swirled it in the sweet and sour sauce, taking a bite before he spoke again, "You know," he held his hand in front of his mouth as he cleared the food away and swallowed. "I don't like this situation either, when I'm around you I want to touch you, and it sucks that I can't always do that."

I sighed and shook my head slightly, "Let's change the subject. This isn't getting us anywhere; neither of us can change the policy."

"I've been thinking though, what if we both changed jobs? We could look for work at two different law firms, that way we can't be affected by 'no dating' policies."

The thought of being free to date openly excited me. I would finally be able to touch him more than once a week.

"That's a great idea. Would it be hard for you to find another job? It's pretty competitive out there isn't it?" I asked.

"My dad's a barrister, remember? He got me this job. He should be able to help me out."

"Oh yeah, I forgot about that. Is he ok with you dating someone from your office?"

"He doesn't know."

"Oh, would he disapprove?" I probed, feeling slightly disappointed that he hadn't mentioned me to his father.

"I don't know. We don't talk about this kind of stuff." His demeanour changed as he shifted in his seat, giving me the impression that he wasn't really interested in talking much about his dad, so I left the subject alone.

"Ok, well I guess I could start looking for a different job next week? – maybe get the paper tomorrow and go through the jobs section."

"So it's settled then?" he asked, a gleam in his eyes as excitement settled in.

"Yes, it's settled - new jobs it is," I agreed as we clinked our glasses together in toast to our newly decided plan.

Turning back to our food we ate quietly for a while. I had no idea what was going through Elliot's head but in mine, I was going over this decision, it meant that things were moving forward for us and becoming a bit more serious.

I knew I was falling hard for Elliot, and I was hoping that he felt the same way about me. I was worried that maybe this thing between us was only this intense because we had to hide it. What if we had met under different circumstances? Would we still be this attracted to each other?

"Would you like to watch a movie tonight?" Elliot asked me, interrupting my thoughts.

"Do you think you can keep your hands off me for that long?" I asked him in a sultry voice.

"I'm not guaranteeing anything," he replied as he got up and took our plates to the sink, rinsing them. "All of the DVDs are in the cupboard next to the TV. You can choose while I clear up in here if you like."

I took my glass of wine with me and walked through to the lounge room, opening the door to peruse the selection of movies. "Do you have any preferences?" I called out to him. The choices were what you would expect from a guy, big blockbuster action movies, some more obscure kung fu type movies and a smattering of documentaries.

"Not really, pick anything you think you'll like," he called back.

Choosing a movie I hadn't seen yet, I put it in the DVD player. I was standing in front of the television trying to work out the remote control when Elliot joined me holding his own glass of wine and the rest of the bottle.

"Which one did you choose?"

"Indiana Jones."

He smiled, remembering our lift encounter, "You still haven't seen that?"

I smiled, "Not yet. I think I chose the first one – I saw there were a few in there."

Elliot glanced over at the case and nodded, indicating that I had made the right choice.

Elliot set the bottle and his glass on the coffee table and sat on the lounge. Joining him, I handed him the remote, snuggling in next to him as he put his arm around me. I rested my head on his chest, listening to the steady rhythm of his heart beating as we watched the movie.

***

I was in the bathroom getting ready to go out the next night after having spent an entire 24 hours with Elliot. As was expected, he got a little frisky through the movie last night, and we didn't quite make it to the end.

We had gone swimming at the Bondi outdoor pool that morning and for once we got to behave like a couple and be a little playful together in the water after we had finished our laps. Spending the rest of the day lying on the beach, talking and playing in the surf before going back to Elliot's flat, making love and falling asleep together - tired out from all the sun.

I sighed contentedly to myself as I ran my straightening iron through my hair. I applied only a small amount of foundation to cover my scar and even out my skin tone, I then added a brush of mascara and some rose coloured lip gloss, dabbing a little on my cheeks as well to give me that flushed girly look.

When I left the bathroom, I found Elliot waiting for me in the lounge room flicking through the channels on the TV. He switched it off as I approached and let out an appreciative whistle. I spun around and posed a little, enjoying the way he looked at me. Being with Elliot did wonders for my self-esteem – if a guy that good looking considered me gorgeous; well, I wasn't going to argue!

I was wearing a black strapless dress covered with small red printed flowers. It had a fitted bodice and a loose flowing skirt that ended just above mid-thigh. I thought it was very feminine and was great for showing off my legs. I topped it off with a pair of red strappy heels.

"You look stunning," Elliot said as he got up and walked towards me, hugging me to him and kissing my neck.

"You're looking pretty gorgeous yourself," I told him, smoothing my hands over his rock-hard chest. He was wearing dark denim jeans that hugged his arse and his package perfectly and an emerald green short-sleeved button up cotton shirt. The muscles in his arms strained against the cuff of his sleeves, I couldn't help but run my hands down his arms to feel the rise and fall of each muscle with my fingertips.

"I think we had better get going before I take you back to bed and throw that dress on the floor," he growled into my ear.

I looked at him in pretend horror, loving every moment that his eyes devoured my body, and his hands wandered over my skin. I doubt I would have fought him if he had carried me to his room and made good on that promise.

"We have to go outside and wait for the cab anyway," he told me taking my hand and leading me to the door. "Do you need to get your purse?"

"No, my ID's in my bra along with my emergency money and ATM card."

He laughed and shook his head, "I'll have to remember that

later."

The cab pulled up almost the second we stepped out of the door. Elliot asked the driver to take us to a nightclub I had never heard of before. He told me that we'd probably see some of his friends there but not to worry because they would love me.

Upon arrival, we walked to the front of the line, and Elliot spoke to the bouncer, shaking hands and sharing a joke with him. The bouncer unclipped the barrier rope and allowed us through, Elliot then told me that he used to work as a bouncer at the club while he was at uni and still knew a few of the guys working there.

Once inside, Elliot asked me what I wanted to drink and lined up at the bar while I scouted a table to sit at. As he was making his way over to me with our drinks, I saw him being stopped by another couple. He was smiling and chatting to them, so I figured they must have been friends of his. Indicating that he was heading over to me, he continued toward me, bringing them over to join us.

I thanked Elliot as he handed me my drink. He leaned close to me, so I could hear him over the music, "Katrina, this is a friend of mine – Gary, and his girlfriend Stephanie. Gary and I went to uni together." I shook hands with both Gary and Stephanie as Elliot yelled to them, "This is my girlfriend – Katrina."

"It's nice to meet you," we all yelled at each other.

Stephanie leaned towards my ear to talk as Elliot and Gary caught up, "Wow, I don't think I have ever met one of Elliot's girlfriends before; you must be pretty special."

I felt myself blush a little, "Oh, I don't know about that."

"So how do you two know each other?"

"We work together."

"Really? I thought Elliot wasn't allowed to date at work."

"Why? Has he wanted to before?"

She laughed and shook her head, "No, I just remember him mentioning it when he started. Gary thought it was a pretty crappy policy."

"Don't we all?! So how long have you known Elliot?"

"A couple of years or so, I started dating Gary when they were in their final year at uni. How about you? How long have you known Elliot?"

"A couple of months. Since I started work."

"And how long have you been dating him?"

"About a month properly, before that we were just getting to know each other."

She nodded, looking thoughtfully at Elliot and Gary talking, "There are going to be a lot of girls around here that are going to hate you for snagging him."

I rolled my eyes and laughed, "Is there anywhere that doesn't have girls crushing on Elliot?"

She laughed again, "I don't think that's possible."

I shrugged my shoulders and gave her a look that said 'well there you go'.

A group of three guys and two girls came over and said hello to Elliot, Gary and Stephanie. It was a flurry of hand clapping, shoulder slapping and cheek kissing. One of the girls lingered with her hand on Elliot's shoulder, and I felt a pang of jealousy in the pit of my stomach. It was short-lived as he reached out for me and brought me to his side, introducing me to the group. I didn't really catch their names, but I nodded hello and shook hands smiling politely, the girl who had been clinging to Elliot gave me a fake bright smile and shook my hand very weakly.

"So this is your local hang out?" I asked Elliot. One of the other guys; I thought his name was Michael – announced that he was buying a round and took off for the bar.

Elliot smiled after him before turning his attention back towards me, "Yeah it is, I've known most of these guys since uni, a couple I know from when I was a bouncer here." He leaned in and briefly kissed me, pulling back to look at me slightly concerned, "You're ok here aren't you? Are you having fun?"

"I'm fine, Elliot – I'm having a good time," I smiled brightly to show him I meant what I said and kissed him back – and I did mean what I said, I was having a good time; it was great to see Elliot in his element as well as to meet his friends. It made me feel more like his girlfriend and less like a dirty little secret.

The guy I thought was called Michael came back to the table with a tray full of tequila shots, a bowl full of lemon wedges and sachets of salt.

"Alright everyone, lick your hands and hold them out," he bellowed over the music, shaking salt on the back of our hands between our thumb and index fingers. One of the others handed out the lemon wedges, and another handed out the tequila shots.

Michael called out "Ready! Go!" and we all licked the salt, knocked back the tequila and sucked on the lemon, dropping the rind back on the tray as we all made noises about how much the alcohol burned on its way down our throats.

"I swear that stuff removes your nose hairs!" yelled Stephanie.

I nodded in agreement. I felt as though my own sinuses were much clearer after that shot.

"Time for another!" one of the other guys called as he came over with a new loaded tray.

"Holy shit!" I said laughing as I was already starting to feel the effect of the alcohol all the way down to my feet.

"You don't have to do them if you don't want to," Elliot assured me.

"It's ok. I'll be fine." Famous last words.

I think we did six shots in total before moving on to drinking vodka mixers, we were all laughing and dancing and just being generally stupid – as you tend to be when thoroughly intoxicated.

The dance floor was packed. It was hot and bodies were pressed against bodies gyrating away to the music under the constant flashing lights. The music was so loud that I could feel it vibrating in my chest.

Elliot and I broke away from the rest of the group. I had my arms wrapped around his neck and was swaying to the music. Grabbing a hold of my head to still my movement, he pulled me towards him, kissing me. Long deep devouring kisses that travelled down my neck and back up to my mouth. I started to get so lost in my body's desire for him that my awareness faltered. I started writhing up against him, feeling him becoming aroused as I rubbed him through his jeans.

I felt a vibration as he moaned into my mouth and pulled my body closer to his, gripping my behind and letting his hand travel under my dress to rub between my legs, I lifted one of my legs and wrapped it around his waist, pressing myself against his erection. He gripped my buttocks tightly and pressed himself harder against me as we continued to move to the music in the middle of a crush of bodies.

With the alcohol removing any concern for what I was about to do, I reached between us and undid his zipper, sliding his erection out and taking it inside me via the side of my panties. We both gasped as we made contact, never breaking the connection between our mouths. I kept my leg up and wrapped tightly around his waist as we moved our hips together – my head was filled with the rush of desire I felt for Elliot, the dizzying effects of the alcohol and the thump of the music; I didn't care where we were, and I didn't spare a thought for getting caught, and obviously neither did he.

He groaned into my mouth as he came, and I experienced a sheer rush of adrenaline, enjoying what it was I did to him; what we did to each other, our desire was hard to control while sober – with us both being drunk, neither of us stood a chance.

I put my leg back down as he slid out of me and straightened himself up as discreetly as possible, he held my face in his hands and grinned wildly at me, laughing and shaking his head before he kissed me again, his expression said 'How do you get me to do these things?' which was becoming a regular thing between us. I laughed with him, as we continued to dance and kiss and touch each other, ignoring everyone else around us.

My mouth had gone dry so I told Elliot I needed some water. He immediately volunteered to go and get me some. Nodding,

I told him I'd meet him at the bar – I needed to visit the ladies' room to clean up after our little tryst. He nodded ok and we went in opposite directions, holding on to each other until we couldn't reach anymore, we couldn't wipe the smiles from our faces.

When I reached the ladies' room, the line was snaking towards the door as it typically did in nightclubs. As I waited I saw Stephanie talking to another girl while she touched up her makeup. Spotting me too, she smiled at me in the mirror. Once she had finished applying her lip gloss, she came over to where I was waiting in the line.

"You look like you've been having a good time!" she cooed at me.

I laughed and nodded as the other girl came and stood beside Stephanie, "So you're Elliot's girlfriend?" she held out her hand to shake mine, "I'm Jasmine," she told me.

"Hi, I'm Katrina," I shook her hand in return.

"So you have to tell us, how did you land Elliot? He never goes out with any of us – not through a lack of trying on our part," Jasmine laughed. "So we're all dying to know how you did it."

"I didn't do anything Jasmine. We just get along."

"Yes but I get along with Elliot too, what makes us so different?" She didn't seem to be saying this to be snide, there was more of a genuine curiosity behind her words. I have to admit that I could see where she was coming from, she really was a gorgeous girl, with dark chocolate eyes, honey kissed hair and full lips. She was probably a head shorter than me and had a classic hour-glass figure that men drool over. I could understand that when you look like her, you are used to having men all over you, so when a guy doesn't give you the attention you are after – it could be a little confronting.

Compared to her, I felt enormous and awkward. I get my fair share of attention from men, but it's rare that I get that attention from someone who is taller than me. Normally, I find that the tall fit men, I am interested in are always attracted to girls who look exactly like the one standing in front of me.

"Jasmine!" Stephanie admonished her.

"What? I'm not being mean, I'm just wondering is all," Jasmine defended herself.

"I'm not offended it's fine. I understand – and seriously, I didn't do anything special; we just get along. We train together at lunch times and everything just kind of progressed from there."

"Ah, see! I knew there had to be something special about you – you're a fitness nut too," she said waggling her finger at me and smiling like she broke the code.

It was my turn to use the toilets, so I told them that I'd see them out there. When I had finished and left the cubicle I almost laughed aloud when I saw my reflection in the mirror. My mouth was all red from all the kissing earlier, and my hair was slightly messed up – I patted some water over my face and wiped a bit of smudged mascara from under my eyes. The girl next to me offered me her lip gloss and I happily accepted, applying it before I smoothed down my hair and teetered back out to the dance floor feeling slow and light headed.

Making my way over to the bar, I couldn't see Elliot. I looked towards the tables we had been sitting at earlier and found him there talking to Michael and Gary. When he saw me, he smiled, holding up the bottle of water he had gotten for me. I walked over to him and took it, gratefully drinking half of it. Waiting for me to screw the lid back on, he pulled me down to sit on his lap, absent-mindedly caressing my thigh as he continued to talk to his friends.

A few others came over to join us, and some of the girls asked me if I wanted to go and dance again while the men all talked and drank. I was about to go, but Elliot tightened his grip around my waist and implored me to "stay" before kissing me behind my ear, my heart flipped with emotion and the intimacy of that one word – wild horses couldn't have dragged me off his lap at that point.

When the club closed we all went outside together, some wanted to continue to party elsewhere while others said their goodbyes and made their way to the taxi rank. Elliot's friends were very complimentary towards me and said they hoped to see me again soon.

Elliot put his arm around me, and we walked over to join the queue so we could catch a taxi back to his place, "Did you have a good time tonight?" he asked me.

"I did. Your friends are really nice. Thanks for introducing me."

"I'm glad you like them. They seemed to like you."

"Well, I think I was a bit of an enigma to them. They said you don't bring girls out very often."

"No, I don't."

"Good," I told him seriously, I didn't think I could have taken it if I was perceived as just another girl hanging off Elliot's arm.

We stopped when we reached the end of the line, and he turned to me, "I'm not hiding my feelings for you anymore Katrina. I don't give a fuck about work anymore. I just care about being with you."

"Really?" In my drunken mind, that was one of the most romantic things anyone had ever said to me. I kissed him, emotion mixed with alcohol swirling within me. It was at that moment, I knew that I had fallen in love with him.

A night of dancing had left my feet aching, so I took my shoes off in the cab and walked up to his flat in bare feet.

We weren't as urgent with each other when we got inside this time, instead he led me to his room, and we took our time, slowly undressing and touching each other. I loved to run my hands over his chest and down over his abs, feeling the hard strength rippling just under his smooth skin.

When he laid me on the bed, he took his weight on his hands and held himself over me looking down, searching my face with his eyes. I smiled, languishing under his gaze as I reached up to run my hands through his thick hair.

"I'm in love with you," he said seriously.

"I'm glad, because I'm in love with you too," I whispered back, my voice too choked with emotion to make any real sound.

He leaned down and kissed me, making love to me so tenderly that I almost cried with the beauty of it. I had never thought that I would be this enraptured with a man again after what had happened with Christopher but here I was feeling like I had no option but to surrender to what I was feeling and let it consume me.

Chapter 19

I'd like to say that the next week we both went and found new jobs, riding off into the sunset together, but that's just not how it was. Instead, when I arrived at work on Monday, I saw that Elliot wasn't in yet. I tried calling him on his mobile and didn't get an answer. Concerned, I called his house, feeling surprised when his father answered.

"Oh, hi, is Elliot there at all?" I asked politely.

"Who's this?" his father demanded.

My heart skittered across my chest nervously, "Um, it's Katrina, is he there?"

"Katrina huh? And who are you to my son Katrina? Because I haven't heard your name before."

I stammered taken aback at his abrasive tone, "I, uh…"

"You wouldn't happen to be the little westie girl he seems so willing to ruin his career over would you?"

I could feel my face burning; this isn't what I had expected when I dialled this number, "Can you just tell him I called please?"

He didn't answer, instead he grunted and hung the phone up in my ear.

The 'westie girl'? Was that man serious? I understood that Western Sydney came with its fair share of stereotypes, but being from there didn't automatically make me classless and uncouth.

I was fuming, feeling agitated I needed to talk to someone about it - David was out of the question, and my mother would panic. My brother would be at work and unable to talk, and I didn't really have any close girlfriends to talk to. I decided my best options were to talk to Kayley, who I trusted, or Carmen, who was in a similar situation to me. Weighing my options, I decided on Carmen and went to her office.

She looked up at me and smiled when I tapped on her door. "Are you busy right now?" I asked.

"No, not really, come on in. Is something wrong?" she asked when she saw the anxious look on my face.

I kept my voice low so any passer-by wouldn't overhear what we were talking about, "Yeah, it's kind of relationship stuff - is that ok? It's just you're the only one who really knows what's going on right now."

"It's fine, Katrina. Why don't you shut the door and take a seat," she told me kindly. I had become quite friendly with Carmen since I had been working here, sometimes catching the train home together in the evenings or stopping by for a chat with each other during work hours. I think it was nice for both of us to have someone around that we could talk freely with.

I told her briefly about how my relationship with Elliot had been progressing and how we had spoken about getting new jobs so the policy wouldn't affect us anymore. I then told her about the conversation with Elliot's father this morning and how he called me a 'westie girl'.

"So, I'm more than a little confused right now. One minute he tells me he loves me and the next he's not answering his phone, and I am getting insulted by his father because I come from Western Sydney. What does he think? That I'm some uneducated low-life who is set upon dragging his son down with me? What the hell difference does it make where I'm from?!"

"Well from what I know Elliot's family has a lot of money. With the exception of his mother, they're all born and bred along the northern beaches and have that upper class mentality at times. I copped it once from one of Andrew's friends, I can't remember what I did, but he said to me 'You can take the girl out of Penrith, but you can't take the Penrith out of the girl.' – I was livid, and I wanted to scratch his eyes out for being such a dickhead; but that would have just proven him right, so I smiled and laughed like it was nothing instead."

"What did Andrew do?"

"Nothing, we had our first major fight over it and almost broke up. Obviously, we didn't and now he defends me with a bit more gusto. Maybe you just need to give Elliot a bit of time to stand up to his dad? He gets a lot of pressure from his father, since he still pays for everything. Junior solicitors don't make a lot of money, so he's still needs his dad to help make ends meet. Just be patient, if he was willing to change everything for you yesterday, I'm sure his feelings haven't changed that much over night."

***

A week later I still hadn't heard from Elliot. I knew he was in the office, but I was so angry at him that I really didn't want to see him. Time was dragging on, and I felt like I was one big ball of pent-up anger, I was angry at Elliot for ignoring me. I was angry at David for avoiding me, and I was angry at myself for getting caught up in my emotions when I had promised myself I wouldn't do that again.

I purposefully took the sorted microfiche to Elliot's office at lunch time, so I didn't have to see him. As I passed Beth's desk, I saw a photo pinned to her cork board – it was of her and David. She was smiling and looking at the camera, and he was kissing her on the cheek. My head started to throb when I saw it, I was so upset with him for leaving me, and I was furious seeing him posing with her. I desperately wanted to rip that photo down, tear it into little pieces and stomp it into the floor.

"We took that at my friend's birthday party last weekend," Beth said behind me.

Taking a calming breath, I plastered a fake smile on my face before I turned around, "It's a great picture," I told her flatly.

"Thank you," she said walking over to it and touching it. "I think we look really good together, don't you?" I could see in her eyes that she was goading me.

"Sure, you look great," I replied quickly. I then held up the microfiche in my hand, walking into Elliot's office and dropping them on his desk.

As I exited Beth called, "I'll tell David you said hi. I'm just about to meet him for lunch."

"You do that," I told her, turning on my heels and walking away from her. What David saw in her, I had no idea.

I desperately needed to get out of the office to clear my head. Grabbing my bag, I caught the lift downstairs. When I stepped out, I saw David lounging on the circular lounge in the foyer. I smiled tightly at him and started directly for the door.

He jumped up, "Katrina, wait a second – is everything ok?" he looked at me, his brows furrowed in concern.

"What the fuck do you care!" I snarled at him over my shoulder, not bothering to stop on my way towards the automatic doors.

He caught me by the arm, stopping me in my tracks. I stopped moving but kept my face turned away from him. I was barely holding myself together and David knew me well enough to read my emotions. I didn't need him to be kind to me – I'd fall apart if he was.

His voice was soft when he spoke, "Trina, just because I need my space right now, doesn't mean I don't care about you."

Tears surged from within me and threatened to spill from my eyes, I swallowed the lump in my throat, forcing my emotions back down inside of me. "Barely speaking to me for a month is a funny way of showing it," I bit back at him, snapping my arm from his grasp and storming out of the door, squeezing my eyes shut to keep my tears at bay.

I spent my lunch time walking at top speed through the streets of the city trying to work away my anger and my disappointment.

When I thought about Elliot or David, I wanted to cry or scream out my rage. David had deserted me and left me friendless when we had spent the majority of our lives being him and me against the world; and then there was Elliot, who had lifted me up and made me love again only to turn cold on me a day later – because why? His dad didn't approve? I could only suppose since he wouldn't even talk to me!

I got back to work late but didn't really care if I got into trouble for it – no one noticed except of course Bianca, who made a comment as I passed reception. I simply glared at her and kept going, not feeling in the mood for her bullshit.

I motored through everything that was in my tray, searched the office for missing books and then asked Priya if I could go home an hour early since there was nothing left for me to do work wise. She agreed, and I grabbed my things, taking the door that led to the bathrooms so I bypassed reception, not wanting to walk past Bianca again.

Instead, I almost walked smack into Elliot; we stopped and stared each other for a moment, both clearly frazzled by walking into each other like that. I narrowed my eyes at him and waited for him to say something. He at least had the decency to appear flustered under my gaze, he looked at his feet and cleared his throat.

"Excuse me," he said quietly, stepping to the side to let me through.

My breath caught as my heart shattered into a million pieces, I couldn't believe he was that cold towards me – there wasn't a person around to see him speak to me kindly; He could have at least told me that he would call so we could talk, or said sorry for not contacting me – something!

"Go and fist yourself," I snarled at him as I passed, if I was going to get dumped for being a westie – I might as well act like one.

That interaction spoke volumes to me and I deserved better, I was done with him.

***

The moment I walked in the front door, I saw my mother and burst into tears. I had been strong and held on to my emotions all day but upon seeing her, the person who loved me most in this world, I couldn't hold on any longer.

She sat with her arm around me and listened as I sobbed out my story, telling her how stupid I felt to get my hopes up when Elliot suggested new jobs so we could be together, and even more stupid for believing him when he told me he loved me. I told her about the short conversation I had with his father and how he'd called me a 'westie girl' and how Elliot had been ignoring my calls and texts and how he acted like he didn't know me - even when no one else was around. I then told her about the photo I saw of David and Beth and how much I felt hurt and abandoned by him – I missed him so much and right now; I felt incredibly small and alone.

My mother didn't give me any advice, she just held me while I wept and then covered me with a blanket when I fell asleep.

Chapter 20

I spent the next week in mourning. Moving through my life like a zombie – performing all of my necessary tasks while my mind could focus on nothing but my troubles. In two short months, I had managed to drive away my best friend because of a relationship with a man who turned the other way and ran the moment things started to move forward.

Each time my phone beeped I jumped and grabbed at it, fiercely hoping for a life line from one of them. Each time I was saddened when instead, it was a text from my mother, with information about dinner or her whereabouts, or my brother sending me a joke to try to cheer me up and occasionally, Christopher. *At least I could manage to keep one guy interested in me,* I thought despondently as I looked down at one of his texts.

I was angry and disappointed with Elliot, but with David, I was angry at myself for not listening to him – again. I felt bad for treating him ruthlessly when I saw him in the foyer at work, but pride, and the fear that I had ruined what little we had left stopped me from trying to contact him.

When I woke on Wednesday morning, I felt empty, and very swollen from another night spent crying and feeling sorry for myself. I went to the freezer and pulled out an ice pack, wrapping it in a tea towel before laying back down to press it over my eyes. My mother made me a cup of sweet milky tea, as she had been every day the last week - saying that it's great for a heart ache; and left me alone again.

I dragged myself into work and once again avoided everyone I could. Carmen had told me on Monday that she had questioned Andrew about why Elliot wasn't speaking to me, and he had told her that Elliot's father had threatened to cut him off entirely if he continued our relationship. As was expected, it all had to do with the fact I was from Western Sydney and that Elliot's father thought that I was only after him for their money.

The thing that hurt me most was that Elliot didn't fight for us, he told me he loved me and wanted to be with me and then the moment his father got involved, he cut off all contact – he didn't even have the decency to break up with me via a text message! He just left it all in the air, unresolved and hanging there. I thought we had enough of a friendship that at the very least I deserved an "I'm sorry, but it's over." But no – there was nothing. He just treated me like he didn't even know me. Gotye's *Somebody that I used to know*, had become my song of the moment, I listened to it repeatedly as my mind worked through my feelings.

I hadn't trained all week as I didn't have the energy to put into it, I was seriously considering giving up the sport altogether to focus more on uni and work – I needed to change my life; it just wasn't working the way it was.

My phone beeped a message, **Can I come over tonight?** It read. The message was from David. Instead of being elated at seeing his name on my screen, I huffed out my breath and dropped my phone on the desk beside me without replying. I had been expecting to feel glad when he contacted me. But after all I had been through recently, seeing his name invoked fear of another heated discussion between us and I had cried enough. I wasn't in the mood for anymore man drama – I just wanted to… I just wanted to forget them both.

I decided that I could do with a night out dancing, even if it was on my own. When I got home I showered, did my hair and makeup and put on a nice dress; my mother gave me a concerned look when I told her my plans.

"Mum, I just want to try to have a bit of fun – I promise not to have more than two drinks ok?"

"Just be careful, I don't like that you're going out on your own. I wish you'd call your brother and see if he wants to go with you."

"I'm going to the Irish pub mum; there will be somebody I know from school or uni there, for sure."

She sighed and nodded, telling me to have a good time.

I could hear the band playing as I pushed my way through the Wednesday night crowd at the Irish pub in Emu Plains and made my way up to the bar. I ordered a Midori, Bacardi and lemonade – the bartender shook his head and told me they weren't allowed to serve doubles anymore.

"Wow, I haven't been here in a while then – just give me a midori and lemonade, and a Bacardi shot then; can you do that?"

He nodded and started mixing my drink. "I'll pay," a familiar male voice said as a hand came over my shoulder passing a twenty dollar note to the bartender.

"Hello Christopher," I said evenly without turning around.

"Katrina, long time no see."

"Well, I have a very good reason for that," I said holding up my forearms and displaying my scars. "Thanks for the drinks," I picked up my glasses and started to walk outside so I could watch the band.

"Katrina, you know I would never intentionally hurt you – it was the drugs, not me."

"Christopher, I don't want any drama tonight. I forgive you for what happened ok - I just want to go and listen to some music, have my drinks and dance a bit; that's all."

Christopher held out his hands in a non-threatening manner, his dark hair falling over even darker eyes. "Hey, I'm not trying to get you to take me back – I just thought we could hang out a bit; Brent and Abby are here - remember how much fun we used to have before everything got so messed up? No pressure, just friends talking. I promise." He flashed his male model smile at me, stark white teeth against his olive skin and I found myself smiling back and nodding. Despite my better judgement, his charm still worked on me. Clapping his hands together satisfactorily, he said, "That's great. They'll be really happy to see you."

"I'd like to see them too actually." I hadn't seen Brent and Abby since Christopher put me in hospital, and they had come to visit me. Abby had tried to talk to me about Christopher's steroid use. I think she was pleading with me to forgive him and not press charges. I liked her a lot. They had kind of been Christopher's, and my couple friends while we were together.

"Oh my goodness! How great to see you!" Abby called out as I approached with Christopher, "it's been so long – how are you?" she asked hugging me.

"I'm fine," I lied, "it's great to see you. I've missed our chats." That was the truth, I had missed talking to Abby, she was one of the few girls I got along well with.

"Me too, tell me about your life right now – what's happening?"

I gave her the version of my life that didn't involve Elliot or David. I asked her if anything new was happening in her life, and she told me she and Brent had been ring shopping as they were planning on getting engaged – organising a romantic way to propose was up to him, but she wanted to make sure he knew exactly what type of ring to choose.

"About time," I told her. "How long have you two been together? Nearly five years now?"

"Yep, almost," offered Brent, "it's time to turn her into an official ball and chain."

Abby playfully tapped him on the arm, and he held his hands up in surrender. I was so busy watching them that I didn't notice David coming up behind me.

He grabbed me forcefully by the arm and growled close to my ear, "What the hell do you think you're doing?"

I snatched my arm back, and turned towards him, "Why do you care? What are you even doing here?"

"I went by your house, and your mum said you came here. I need to talk to you," he told me.

Christopher moved closer to me and asked protectively, "Is everything alright here?"

I held my hand up and said, "It's fine Christopher. We're just talking."

At the same time, David growled, "Don't even speak to me, Christopher, if it was up to me, you'd be in prison right now, so just fuck the hell off!"

"What did you say to me?" Christopher demanded through clenched teeth, leaning threateningly towards David.

"I said 'fuck. the hell. off' you pussy-hating woman-basher," David goaded, speaking close to Christopher's face.

My mouth fell open as Christopher's fist connected with David's jaw and sent David sprawling on the ground. Christopher then jumped on top of David and started pounding him in the face.

I rushed over and tried to pull him off but only succeeded in getting clipped in the cheek by an elbow as Christopher pulled his fist back to hit David again. I yelped as I stumbled backwards. Brent jumped in along with some random guy I didn't know, and hauled Christopher off David, who was lying on the ground covered in blood and laughing, of all things.

I rushed over to David and knelt down beside him, scowling at Christopher, "Jesus, Christopher! I let you back in my life for five minutes, and you beat the crap out of someone. You know, I believed you when you said it was the drugs, but now I'm thinking you're just a thug! Don't ever speak to me, David or anyone I care about again - or I promise you I will press charges against you for what you did to me."

He looked at me disheartened as he aggressively shrugged the men off who were holding him back. When he started to leave, Brent and Abby followed him out, Abby turning to me and saying, "I am so, so sorry that just happened."

I shook my head to say 'don't worry about it' and turned my attention back to David, who was now trying to sit up.

"What the hell was that David?" I asked him softly. My anger had evaporated the moment, he hit the ground. Accepting a paper napkin from a girl at a nearby table, I held it under his bleeding nose, "He could have killed you, then what would I do?"

David sighed and shook his head, "I don't know. I just saw him near you and pretty much stopped thinking from that point on."

I reached up and moved his hair away from his forehead, "Do you think you have a concussion?"

He started to try and stand up, so I jumped up first to help him. "I don't know," he said. "But I'm pretty sure he broke my nose." The bleeding wasn't slowing down so I grabbed some more napkins to help stem the flow.

"Come on, I'll take you to the hospital and get you checked out."

We walked out to the parking lot together and got into my car, driving in silence to the emergency room at Nepean Hospital.

We were sent through to triage fairly quickly; they assessed the urgency of David's wounds and decided to take him straight through as he was bleeding quite profusely.

I went through with him and sat quietly while one of the nurses cleaned him up. A doctor came by to look at David's face and order some scans to be done to check the extent of his injuries.

When the doctor left the curtained area David turned to me, confusion in his eyes, "Why were you even with Christopher anyway?"

"I wasn't with him. I was actually there talking to Abby – I wanted to go out, and they were there so I was saying hi. It was no big deal, I wasn't trying to rekindle anything."

He reached out to me and took my hand, pulling me towards the bed he was on. I sat down facing him. He kept his eyes focused on my hands as he spoke, "I lost my mind today seeing you with him Katrina," he looked up at me, and I could see the pain in his eyes. "I can't handle seeing you around other guys anymore – especially him." He reached up and touched my cheek gently, "Does this hurt?"

I closed my eyes against his touch, feeling the warm familiarity of his fingers against my skin. I held his hand against my cheek and let a tear escape as my heart ached from missing him so much. I shook my head no, not trusting my voice to speak.

He moved his thumb to wipe my tear away and sat up so his swollen face was closer to mine, "Katrina...I can't handle seeing you with anyone else because... because *I* want to be with you," he whispered. I met his eyes and could see the truth in them. Eyes that were blue like mine and filled with all of the pain and suffering that I had also been feeling during our time apart.

I saw myself in his eyes, there was a connection between us that ran so deeply, we were one and the same. I realised that connection, it had been there all along. "I love you Katrina," he murmured as he moved closer and kissed me gently, softly brushing his swollen lips over mine being careful to avoid hitting his nose.

When he pulled away, he looked into my eyes, his own filled with concern as he wiped at tears I hadn't felt flowing. That was the moment I understood - the entire time I had been with Elliot, I had been missing David. I had felt a like a part of my soul was gone when he wasn't in my life, and I was using Elliot to fill that gaping hole. I didn't love Elliot. I loved David.

My tears flowed more freely now as I admitted to myself what I had been denying for years. *I* loved David – that's why I teased him constantly about the girls he flirted with. That's why I was so angry about Beth; I wanted him to flirt and be with me.

"Hey, baby girl – why are you crying so much? The kiss wasn't that bad was it?" he cooed.

I shook my head and tried to dry my face with my hands. "It was beautiful David. I'm crying because, well, because I love you too, and I have been so miserable without you," I sobbed.

He took me in his arms, and I clutched myself to him crying on his shoulder. He smoothed my hair and shushed me, whispering to me that everything would be alright and that he wouldn't leave me again. He told me how sorry he was, and that he had loved me so much it hurt to be away from me.

A nurse came around and took David to get his scans done, I was told to sit in the waiting room as it was likely he would go home afterwards. A good two hours later David came through the doors with a prescription for painkillers and an information sheet about concussions. The scans didn't show anything except for a fractured nose which was less than we were expecting, but it was still possible that David had a concussion, so he needed to be monitored overnight and wasn't allowed to drive the next day.

I looked at his face, all swollen and bruising already. "Aren't they going to put anything on your nose?" I asked him concerned.

He took me by the hand, "Nah, they said to ice it, and take some painkillers and decongestant. It's just a fracture and should heal fine on its own. But," he grinned that half dimpled grin of his and said, "you're going to have to keep me up all night to make sure I don't have a concussion."

"Well we have a month of catching up to do. I think I can manage that," I told him squeezing his hand.

I drove him back to his house and his mother almost fainted when she saw him. After telling her what happened, I asked her if it was ok if I stayed with him to keep an eye on him for concussion symptoms. Reluctantly she agreed, hovering close by trying to take care of her son herself.

We got David settled in bed after he took his medication and gave him an ice pack for his nose. I called my mother to let her know I was staying at David's place, I told her briefly what happened and despite some pretty heavy sighing, she was reasonably good about it.

I sat down on the bed and tucked my leg underneath myself, so I could face David and talk to him. "So, where do we go from here David?"

"Forward… together," he answered quietly, taking the ice pack off his own face and pressing it to my cheek while he ran his fingers through my hair on the other side.

"What about Beth? What are you going to tell her? She already hates me enough as it is. Her and Bianca will probably string me up for stealing you away."

"I broke up with Beth last week," he said, taking a hold of my hands.

"Last week?"

"Yes, when I saw you upset last Wednesday, I knew I was being unfair to Beth. I guess I was using her to prove that I could move on from you – but I couldn't. I guess it's why I've never really had a relationship; because I've always had you. Although, your friendship isn't enough for me anymore Trina, I want all of you." He moved forward and was about to kiss me when I pulled back.

"I scared of hurting your face," I told him.

"It'll be worth it," he told me, closing the distance between us and kissing me. His kiss was gentle at first but became more insistent as I relaxed into him and allowed his tongue to explore my mouth. He winced when we pressed a little too firmly, but mostly it was one of the most soul warming kisses I had ever experienced, all the emotion and desire my body had been harbouring for him for all those years had been released and was surging through me, setting my skin abuzz as every part of me longed for his touch.

His hands were roaming over my body. "Lock the door," he whispered in my ear.

I got up smiling at him coyly and went and over to turn the lock. We kept watching each other, not really sure who was the hunter and who was the prey.

"Take off your clothes," Ok, I was the prey - his voice was husky as he spoke and his boldness sent a bolt of lust straight between my legs.

I'd never been commanded to take my clothes off before. I had to admit it was hot. He watched me with darkening eyes as I reached behind my back and undid the zipper of my dress, letting it fall off my shoulders exposing my breasts. I could hear his breathing change as watched me shimmy out of it, taking my panties off with it to stand before him, naked, exposed and loving his eyes on my body.

"You are exquisite Trina," he breathed as he held his hands out beckoning for me to come closer. I moved to him, and he pulled me onto the bed kissing me while he ran his hands up and down my naked back, "Lay down," he instructed.

I reclined on the bed in front of him, and he reached up to smooth his hands over my skin, starting from my collar bone and running his fingers down, in between my breasts and over my stomach. He brushed his fingers through the hair on my mound and guided my legs, so I was lying in front of him with my legs open, baring myself to him.

My breathing was hot and heavy as I watched him trace his fingers over my body. He slipped a finger in between my folds, and I gasped when he pushed into me. "Oh, that's wonderful," he whispered, "that's my heaven in there," he said as he moved his fingers in and out of me and started to slide them over my clit and back inside me again. Small whimpers kept escaping my lips as feelings of ecstasy were flooding through my nerve endings.

My orgasm was building quickly, but I wanted more. I wanted - "I want you inside me David," I gasped out, trying to hold out but only managing a few seconds before I exploded around his hand, bucking my hips as I instinctively closed my legs, squeezing myself around him and riding his hand with the waves of my orgasm.

I sat up and reached to unbutton his pants, "I want you inside of me," I said to him more forcefully this time. He grinned that wicked grin of his and lifted his hips to assist me in taking his pants off. I raised my eyebrows as I realised there were just pants. "You don't wear underwear?" I asked him.

He shook his head slowly from side to side, watching me with a half grin.

Being careful to make sure I didn't hurt his face any more than it already was, I lifted his shirt. He raised his arms above his head to aid me and I dropped it on the floor as my eyes wandered over his naked body.

I had seen his chest before, it was lean and fairly well toned with only a light smattering of brown hair over it. He had broad shoulders and long sinewy limbs, and his manhood – well, let's just say it was sizeable.

My mouth dropped open upon seeing it, and I looked up at his eyes. They were dancing with amusement. "It's fine," he assured me, "you'll stretch."

"I hope so," I said eyeing him off as he applied a condom.

"Come," he said guiding me to straddle him, "you control it."

I poised myself above him and took him in my hand, sliding his tip back and forward between my folds to gauge the fit a little. I settled him at my entrance and pressed down a little, gasping as I felt myself expand around him. I moved back up to assist my lubrication and then slid back down, a little further this time.

I let out a shaky breath as I slowly took in his length, feeling him pressing deep inside me. My core quivered at his touch. I was stretched around him, filled completely and the sensation was amazing. I was letting out small whimpers of pleasure as I rode him, grinding our hips together to accept him into the depths of me.

He placed his hands on my hips and stilled me, "Stop, st-st-stop," he breathed out carefully and closed his eyes for a moment, frowning slightly.

"What's wrong?" I panted out, worried I was hurting him.

"Nothing, I just don't want this to end yet."

He winced as I clenched around him, taunting him. "Oh my

god, you're gonna get it," he threatened, grabbing my legs and flipping me back so he was on top of me, still connected.

I laughed. "That was a suave move," I told him.

He closed his eyes and tilted his head in a show of modesty. "Well, I practised these things so I was the best lover possible when you were ready for me."

I feigned horror and slapped his chest lightly, "Is that your story now is it?"

He grunted in the affirmative and tilted his head down to run his tongue around my nipple, blowing lightly on it so it stood up from the cool air and then flicked his tongue over it, sending shivers rippling all over my body. I inhaled sharply as he started to move inside me again.

My eyes rolled back in my head as he filled me so thoroughly. I was experiencing that fine line between pleasure and pain as I protracted around him, and he increased his rhythm. With each thrust, I let out my breath, trying desperately not to make any sound to alert his mother to what we were doing.

When he came I felt his pulsating inside of me and shuddered in response, clenching myself around him once more, shocking us both when it caused me to orgasm for the second time that night.

We lay together, breathing heavily and touching each other, not wanting the closeness to end. We had waited so long to be together that it seemed that now we were connected. We didn't ever want to break apart.

Eventually though, we did, as he withdrew from inside me I felt as though I had this gaping hole between my legs. I squeezed my internal muscles to try to make it feel normal again, but it just felt big and swollen.

I looked up at him concerned, "It's not going to stay stretched is it?" I asked.

He laughed and kissed me on the forehead, "No, not at all. Although you will get used to it – or so I'm told anyway."

He sat back on the bed and held his arms out to me. I slid in beside him and curled up against him as he squeezed his arms around me and said, "I love you more than anything in this world you know. I don't ever want to go through this past couple of months again."

I sighed, "Me either. I felt like a piece of me had gone missing without you in my life. It was like you died, and I couldn't stand it. I tried being angry at you, but that only really made me reckless and horribly sad."

"Reckless, hey? Did you go around stealing cars in my absence?" he joked.

"No, I opened my heart to the wrong person," I felt him stiffen a little as he reached up and smoothed his hand over my hair.

"Did he hurt you at all?" he asked flatly, a slight chill to his words.

"Only my pride, I was mostly upset about not being able to talk to you." I sat up and looked him in the eye, so he could see my face as I said this, "I love you David. You are more a part of me than I am."

"I am the same," he whispered emotionally as he pulled me to him and kissed me again. I reached my hand up and smoothed it gently over the side of his face, feeling the dampness of tears. I sat back from him and wiped at his tears as softly as I could. He reached up in turn and tried to wipe away the tears I had been shedding.

"Aren't we a pair!" I exclaimed, "getting all emotional after making love." I smiled at him weakly, my lip trembling as fear gripped at my heart, "I am scared that this is a dream. I'm petrified that I will wake up at home, and you still won't be talking to me," I whispered to him, my eyes wide and serious.

"It's no dream baby girl," he told me gently, holding my face so he was looking straight into my eyes. "How about we try to get some sleep? That way, you will wake up here and know that this," he used his hands to emphasise our connection, "is real."

I nodded my head, "Ok," I got up and went over to his alarm clock. "How often do I have to wake you up?"

"You don't have to. It's been hours, and I'm fine. I'm sure some sort of symptom would be showing by now," he said calmly. "Come to bed Trina, sleep with me."

I padded back to his bed and climbed in, resting my head on his chest as we held each other tightly, "I'm sorry your nose is broken," I said to him.

"It's not, it's fractured," he replied to me. "I'm sorry your cheek is bruised." He ran his fingertips up and down my side as he planted a kiss on my head. "Get some sleep Trina, I promise I will still love you in the morning and then every morning after that."

Chapter 21

"I've got something for you," David said, moving over to his desk and opening the drawer. When he turned he was holding a small box.

"But it's not Christmas for a couple of weeks yet!" I exclaimed. I sucked my breath in a little, excited by this impromptu gift. It was Friday morning and I was still in my pyjamas, sitting in the middle of his bed with my legs crossed. He came to sit in front of me before presenting me with a thin navy blue rectangular shaped box, tied with a white ribbon.

I held it in my hand for a moment, trying to guess what it was. "Open it," he urged me.

Pulling at the ribbon, I let it fall either side of my hand. David was watching me eagerly as I slid off the lid and placed it on the bed beside me. White tissue paper was covering the gift and when I moved it aside there sat a silver necklace with a spinning disc attached to it. On one side were the letters 'L V Y U' and on the other, 'I O E O'.

I looked at David curiously, not understanding what the letters were. "Spin it," he said, his eyes twinkling and the corner of his mouth turning up with enjoyment as he watched me.

I did as I was told and held the necklace up, so I could see the disc more closely. As it spun the letters came together and spelled 'I LOVE YOU'. My chest swelled, and tears pricked my eyes as I was touched by the thoughtfulness of his gift. I looked from the necklace to David, who was biting his lip, waiting for my response.

"Oh David," I breathed, "this is the most beautifully corny gift anyone has ever given me. I love it! I love you!" I crawled forward on the bed and sat in his lap with my legs wrapped around his waist, kissing him tenderly to show my gratitude for such a beautiful gift. "Thank you so much, I'll wear it always."

"You're more than welcome," he whispered as he took it from me and started undoing the clasp. "I wanted to get you something to commemorate our first month as a couple." I held my hair up as he reached behind me, re-joining the clasp and adjusting the necklace so it sat neatly on my breastbone.

I fingered the disc, twirling it as I smiled happily at him, "A whole month hey? That's got to be a bit of a record for you – I'm honoured." His longest relationship so far had been with

Beth, and that had lasted for only three weeks.

"Hey, why would I want to spend a whole month in the company of another girl when I have always had you?" he tackled me on the bed and started getting frisky, I reached up and touched his, now healed face affectionately.

"I love you David, and I love my gift," I whispered to him again.

He nibbled at my ear and whispered, "I love you too Trina," before he sat back and took his shirt off.

I looked at the clock, "Do we have time for this?" I asked, knowing that we both had a train to catch so we would get to work on time.

"We do if we're quick," he said grinning wickedly as he whipped my pyjama shorts down my legs.

Half an hour later I was satisfied, showered, dressed and at the kitchen table having breakfast chatting with David's mother.

"I am so glad you two got back together," she said to me after inspecting the necklace David had bought me.

"*Back* together? This is the first time we've actually been a couple, before that we were just friends Mrs Taylor," I told her feeling a little confused. I thought she had always been clear on our relationship status.

"No, you were together, you've always been together – you just didn't know it at the time. I could see the way you were around each other, and I know my David. He's been in love with you for as long as he has known you."

David walked out of the bathroom at that moment, bringing the scent of soap and steam with him, passing by and kissing me on the head before he took a seat at the table next to me. "Did you see what I got Trina, Ma?" he asked as he crushed weetbix into his bowl.

"I did, it's beautiful," she said smiling. "I was just telling Trina how glad I am to see you both so happy."

He poured his milk and sprinkled sugar while he nodded and grinned uncontrollably, "It's true. I've never been happier."

"You should have seen him for that month you two weren't getting along. That big grin of his was nowhere to be seen, and I swear he lost a good two inches in height moping around the place with his lip out," she teased.

"It's true, my soul was torn in two," he said dramatically through a mouthful of cereal.

I laughed at him and playfully nudged into him, "Well if it wasn't for that month, we probably wouldn't have had this month."

"You're probably right. We'd probably still be in 'best friend land' if it hadn't been for me getting insanely jealous when I saw you with that Elliot guy," he admitted, chewing thoughtfully. "Has he even spoken to you yet or is he still avoiding you?"

"Still avoiding me – the last thing I said to him was 'go fist yourself' so I think it's pretty clear to him where I stand on everything."

"Katrina! You didn't say that!" Mrs Taylor gasped almost choking on her coffee.

"I did. I was furious with him for not having the decency to at least dump me." I saw the questioning look on Mrs Taylor's face, so I filled her in. "His father threatened to take his precious money away if he didn't stop dating me – because as far as he was concerned a westie girl wasn't good enough for his son. Instead of breaking up with me Elliot just cut off all contact."

"Well how did you find out what happened if he's been ignoring you?" she asked, understandably.

"Chinese whispers," David said knowingly.

"No, not Chinese whispers – a girl I know at work is dating one of his friends; she found out and told me."

"Yeah, Chinese whispers," David repeated.

"It doesn't matter anyway; he doesn't sound like a very good person if he can just stop talking to you with no explanation," Mrs Taylor added as she got up and took her dishes to the kitchen.

David put his arm around me and hugged me to him, "Well, if it wasn't for him, we probably wouldn't have our shit together. At least now, we don't have to worry about anyone else hurting you though, right?"

"That's right. You're my world, my forever," I said dramatically, laughing as I kissed him lightly on the mouth.

"Erk! You two are giving me a toothache you're so sweet," Mrs Taylor put in from the kitchen. She looked at her watch, "I have to go, or I'll miss my train. Are you two staying here tonight or at Katrina's place?"

"I have my work Christmas party tonight, and then we're going out afterwards," I told her. "So we might go back to my place because we'll be late and my mum and dad sleep like the dead. We won't disturb them coming in."

"Ok, well I'll see you both over the weekend sometime?" I nodded as she held her hand up in goodbye and walked out the front door.

David looked at me with a mischievous grin on his face, "What?" I asked.

"We don't need to come home this weekend," he told me, his eyes sparkling.

"Why not?"

"Because, I got us a room in the city for two nights - we can stay there all weekend."

"Oh my god! You're amazing." I threw my arms around his neck and hugged him tightly, kissing him on the cheek.

"I thought it would be nice not to worry about parents for a weekend."

"Have I told you today that I love you?"

"You have, but keep saying it; I like the way it sounds."

I told him again and kissed him passionately, breathing him in.

"Let's go before we miss our train," I suggested pulling away before we ended up in the bedroom again.

Chapter 22

"I love half days," Kayley said as she approached my desk. "Are you looking forward to your first work Christmas party?"

I wrinkled my nose, "I don't know. I'm a bit nervous actually."

"Don't be, they're great – they are pretty swanky and everybody gets drunk and starts dancing and letting loose. Then we are all going out afterwards so it's a day and night full of fun, fun, fun!"

"Let me guess. You're going out to Pontoon afterwards?"

"Hell yeah, we all love it there, there's dancing, food, billiards and best of all – couches. I just love the couches. Are you coming this time? You've been notably absent these past couple of months."

"Well, it's a bit uncomfortable being around Beth these days. So I thought it best to stay away."

Kayley laughed, "You know her and Bianca only come out with us when you're there, they normally have nothing to do with us."

"Really?" I said taken aback slightly.

"Yep," she drummed her hands on the top of my partition, "Well, I'm off – do you want me to go downstairs with you and show you where the bus picks us up?"

"That would be great Kayley, thanks."

When the time came to leave, the entire office stood on the side of the road and waited for the two buses the company had hired to safely ferry us all to the Park Hyatt. The function room was beautifully appointed with round tables covered in white linens and festive silver and blue centrepieces, surrounding a buffet and a small dance floor.

Christmas music was crooning out of the speakers and waiters were circulating with trays of wine and beer. There was a bar at the back of the room that served spirits for you to buy and soft drinks, which were free.

I took a glass of wine from one of the trays and walked

towards the nearest table to inspect the settings. I noticed there were name cards at each table telling us where to sit.

"Oh god, I hope I'm not seated next to my boss," Kayley said from beside me, "I'm going to find out where I am and move my name if I'm not happy." She gave me a mischievous look before dashing off to find her name.

I really wasn't fussed about where I was sitting and spent a bit of time chatting to a few people I knew and admiring the Christmas decorations around the room. They were all white faux pine with silver and royal blue decorations, the light in the room had a blue hue to it as well and they were pumping that smoke they use in night clubs into the room at floor level, creating a very misty swirl as everyone moved around.

"So what do you think of it all?" Carmen asked as she approached me smiling warmly.

"It's lovely, almost – magical," I breathed looking around, "I think this is the fanciest place I've ever been to."

"Me too, they go all out don't they?"

I nodded, still looking around the room, feeling like I had entered some kind of Christmas wonderland.

"Have you found your name card yet?" she asked me.

"No, I've been too busy admiring the room."

"Well, you had better claim your seat fast, people are rearranging the cards – you'll get stuck next to someone awful if you're not quick enough," she warned me.

I laughed, "Well in that case. I'd better get moving."

I wished Carmen a good time and started to make my way around the tables trying to find my name. A lot of people had already taken their seats and were chatting happily. I spotted Kayley already seated and she signalled to me that she didn't know where my name was.

My heart fell when I finally found my name. I hadn't even considered the possibility of placed there. I was seated on the right-hand side of Elliot, to his left was Beth and to her left was Bianca. There were eight people to a table and two others, that I didn't know, were sitting across from me. I stood back from the table a little, not really wanting to sit down just yet.

Ken, the partner I had spoken to at drinks, stood up at the front of the room tapping the microphone to get everyone's attention, "If everyone could please find their seats. The buffet will soon start, then we'll have some speeches, a few fun awards and a bit of dancing when the eating is all done."

I rolled my eyes and huffed out my breath as I moved forward and roughly dragged my chair out to sit down. I didn't bother looking at the three that I already knew. I just smiled and nodded at the four I didn't know, introducing myself to the person who had come to sit at my right. He was softly spoken, and I struggled to hear him over the noise of the room but I thought he introduced himself as Eric.

"Long time no see," Elliot murmured in my ear.

Turning slowly, I levelled my gaze on him, and I could see his eyes darken. He still set off the primal responses in my body but I didn't have that same need or want for him when I looked at him now. "Well, I have been avoiding you. I thought that was what you wanted," I shot quietly back at him, fixing a saccharine smile on my face as I did so.

"No, it's not what *I* wanted, my father..."

"I don't want to hear it. This isn't the time or the place to be having this conversation Elliot," I flicked my eyes to Beth and Bianca, noting their tilted heads as they strained their ears in an effort to hear what we were saying.

"Who cares about those two!" he burst out, louder than he

should. "What are they going to do? Dob on us for talking?"

That's when it dawned on me, "Did you move my name card here on purpose?"

His eyes flicked to the place card in front of me before settling on my own again. "I needed to talk to you," he admitted.

"Here? You couldn't just pick up the phone?"

"Would you have answered if I did?"

I opened my mouth to say yes but shut it abruptly when I realised that no, I probably would have let it ring out. So I answered, "That first week yes, but now – no I wouldn't have."

"See?" he pointed out.

"Fine Elliot, talk – but understand that it will change nothing."

He nodded his head towards Beth, "I heard that you're with David now, I guess there was something to worry about there after all," he commented.

"Who knows Elliot, maybe I would have sacrificed my friendship with David for you – things were fairly intense between us, I thought I loved you. But…" I shook my head and shrugged my shoulders to indicate that we'll never know.

His eyes skimmed over me, and he grunted slightly. I turned my head away from him when it was announced that the buffet was being served. Tables were being called up one at a time to choose their meals.

Letting out my breath, I turned back to him, "So is that why you moved me here? So you could question me about David?"

He shook his head, "No, I'm sorry – it's really none of my business anymore; I'm the one that ruined things, so I was out of line there. I just… I just wanted to talk to you and explain myself. I want to say how sorry I am."

"Elliot, there's nothing to explain – I already know that your father threatened to cut you off for dating a western suburbs girl; I obviously wasn't worth fighting for and that's fine – I accept that. But I think I will be forever pissed at you for giving me the silent treatment instead of having the decency to break it off with me."

He looked down at his hands, "I know. I went about it all wrong, and I'm so sorry for that. I guess I just knew that if I spoke to you; I wouldn't be able to go through with it, and then I'd be out on my own." He spoke quietly like he was a small child. When I used to look at Elliot, I saw a man who had his life together and everything going for him; now I saw him as a boy who was petrified of going against his father.

"I don't know what to say to you Elliot, I'm sorry that your father's money holds such importance to you that you let it rule your decisions. I've never had lots of money so to me; the choice to follow my heart would have been easy." I shook my head, searching for the words to convey how I felt about everything that had happened between us, "You hurt me a lot, Elliot. You made me feel special, you told me you loved me; you let me love you and then poof," I used my hands to mime the word, "it was all gone and all I got was an insult about being a westie from your father and not so much as a text message from you. That hurt me greatly, Elliot, it broke my heart. But it's you, I feel most sorry for," he knitted his brows together as he listened to me. "You're the one that lost out here Elliot. You gave up what you thought was love, for money, money Elliot! I just can't understand that."

"I'm sorry Katrina," he barely whispered. His hand twitched toward mine, but he seemed to realise what he was doing and curled his fingers underneath instead, "I can't tell you enough how sorry I am. You don't know how many times I started to call you, how many times I wrote an email... I know things have changed for you, but my feelings are still the same – I fucked up, I fucked up big time; and I can't change that now, I wish I could, but - I can't," his handsome face was etched with pain as he spoke to me.

Our table got called to go up to the buffet, and the others around us stood to make their way over, leaving Elliot and I on our own for a moment. I watched Beth and Bianca hesitate as they stood, desperately wanting to stay to try to find out what Elliot and I were talking about. I stood as well turning to Elliot, who was still sitting.

"I am really sorry too Elliot, what we had was really special to me. Just be thankful this all happened early on while we were only getting started. At least we weren't too invested in each other yet. Things would have been a lot harder the longer we were together." I touched him lightly on the shoulder and started to make my way to the buffet, but he caught my hand and held me there.

"I'm *still* invested in you," he said looking at me sincerely.

I pulled my hand from his. "I'm sorry Elliot, but I'm not." Walking away from him, I ignored the watchful eyes of others, chancing a glance back towards him when I reached the buffet. He was sitting sideways in his chair slouched over with his elbows on his knees, and his hands clasped together as he stared at the floor. He took a deep breath and sat up, running his hands over his face and through his hair. I decided then that I was going to resign from this job, now fully understanding the reason for the 'no dating' policy – it's hard to be around someone you once loved, even harder to work with them.

As I watched him walk over to the buffet, he gave me a small smile and shrugged his shoulders in capitulation; it was then that I made my next decision – to forgive him. He was clearly torturing himself over what happened, whether I continued to be angry at him or not was really of no consequence anymore. It was time that I looked on our relationship for what it was - a beautiful struggle; one that we ultimately lost, but it was wonderful and all-consuming while it lasted. I couldn't hate him for that.

I got through the necessary parts of the Christmas party trying to talk pleasantly to everyone at my table. Even attempting some nice conversation with Beth and Bianca – I got scowls in response but, at least I tried to make the best of things.

When everyone started dancing I slipped outside to call David and tell him what had just happened.

"Are you ok?" he asked when I was finished, concern edging his voice.

"I'm fine, I actually feel a lot better about everything now. I guess I just needed some closure, you know?" I told him.

"I'm glad you got the chance to talk to him, Trina," he said sincerely.

"Thank you David, I'm glad too."

"Although I do feel sorry for the guy."

"Why is that?"

"Because you're a hard woman to get over Trina. I tried - and I failed miserably"

I laughed through my nose, "You're sweet."

"You're beautiful," he cooed down the line, setting the butterflies in my stomach a flutter.

"I'd better get back in there, I'll see you tonight?"

"You will, I'll call you when I'm finished. Love you."

"Love you too," I smiled as I hung up the phone and went back inside to re-join the party, feeling much lighter now that I had spoken to my best friend, my love.

Epilogue

After I left Turner Barlow & Smith, I went to work at a much smaller law firm as an office all-rounder. I loved it there, getting to do some paralegal work and have a lot more hands-on experience before I finished my degree. I was offered a full-time position when I graduated and became junior solicitor specialising in family law, although being in a small law firm – I was called upon to help out in other areas as well.

David was taken on full time where he had been working as well. We were both moving forward in our career and our relationship, pooling our funds so that we could get a very small and crappy flat, as close to the city as we could afford. It was cramped and a constant mess, but we loved it.

I had given up triathlons after a less than stellar performance at uni that semester I was working and dealing with my personal issues.

I still trained to maintain my fitness and it was whilst out running during my lunch break that I saw Elliot again after almost two years of no contact.

Waving when he saw me, he excused himself from the slightly overweight man he was with and trotted over to me. He looked exactly as I remembered him, his hair was perhaps a little longer but everything else was still the same. As he got closer I noticed that his shirt advertised a personal training company.

"What's this?" I asked him immediately, forgetting to start with 'hi, it's been ages. How have you been?'

He looked down and laughed, "I'm a personal trainer now."

I did a double take, "What? What about becoming a barrister?"

He continued to smile and shook his head. "That was my father's dream for me. After you left, I did a lot of soul-searching and decided to make my own path."

"Wow, that's amazing Elliot. I'm really happy for you."

"Looks like congratulations is owed to you as well," he said nodding towards the engagement ring on my left hand. "Is that from David?" I nodded briefly. David had proposed the night we graduated, and I had gladly accepted.

"Oh thank you, the wedding is a while off, but everything else is great." He smiled forlornly and met my eyes, "How about you? How are things with you?"

A sadness seemed to linger just behind his eyes as he searched my face in the moments before he answered. "Well, I don't really speak to my dad anymore – which really is a good thing; and I'm seeing someone now. It took a while – and she's not you... but things are ok. I'm certainly not ready for a commitment like that yet," he laughed uneasily, nodding at my ring again.

I could see the man Elliot was training standing away from us with his hands on his hips puffing and looking over. "Well, I had better let you get back to it. It was nice to see you again Evan."

He laughed, it had been a long time since I had called him that, but there was little humour in the sound. "You too Katrina. I'll see you around, if not – have a great life!" He gave me a despondent half smile and ran off, returning to his client. I watched him gracefully run away from me, feeling friendly affection and a slight sadness for him before I continued on my way.

Seeing me again was obviously still hard on Elliot, I was so glad that he finally stood up to his father. He did it too late to make any difference to his and my relationship but at least when the next time he found love, it wouldn't matter what her address was.

I looked at the ring that David had given me and remembered how he had proposed. The jewellery box was underneath his graduation cap and when I came over to him with my degree in hand, he had started complaining that his hat was hurting and asked me to check it for him. When he removed his hat and handed it to me; I noticed the box and looked at his face, wondering if it was what I thought it was.

With quivering hands, I opened it, gasping as he got down to his knee and asked me to marry him. I burst into happy tears and said yes, holding my still shaking hand out for him to slide the ring onto my finger. Our families were around us to witness the moment along with a few others from the ceremony, applauding when we kissed each other. It was corny and beautiful and so very David.

As I continued to run along the path, I thought about all the events that had led me to where I was now, my relationship with Christopher, spending time with Elliot and discovering my love for David; it was a difficult and very emotional time, but it got me where I was, so I wouldn't change a thing, not for all the money in the world.

The end… or is it?

A Note from the Author:

Thank you for reading *A Beautiful Struggle*. It might please you to know that I am currently working on Elliot's story. Keep an eye on my blog for progress reports and a release date.

I would love it if you could find the time to review this book on Amazon and/or Goodreads – I love to hear from readers, it helps me become a better writer!

For updates or to ask questions/ send comments,

you can contact me at **lillianaanderson@live.com.au** ,

visit my website & blog at

 http://lillianaanderson.weebly.com/

connect with me on Goodreads

http://www.goodreads.com/author/show/6533406.Lilliana_Anderson

follow me on twitter **@Confidante_Lili**

or facebook

 http://www.facebook.com/lilliana.anderson.12/

http://www.facebook.com/ABeautifulStruggleLillianaAnderson

Once again, I thank you for reading. This is my second book and I plan to write many more.

Lilliana Anderson

Made in the USA
Lexington, KY
07 June 2013